日常英文書信寫作指南

在職場無往不利、在朋友圈有求必應的 36 堂寫作課

從 #請 #謝謝 #對不起 三大情感表達切入，掌握基本原則，寫出各種需求！

1 好禮貌運動，從請、謝謝、對不起開始

LETTER ❶

B U S I N E S S 商務篇

When a Client Ignores You or Disappears into Thin Air...

當客戶忽略你或消失時……

本書共分三大部分：**Part1 請**、**Part2 謝謝**、**Part3 對不起**，分別收錄「**商務篇**」六單元及「**熟人篇**」六單元，帶你學習各種場合的書信表達。

2 讓你脫穎而出的寫作提點

商務篇的「小建議大思考」及熟人篇的「小提醒大領悟」，提醒你書寫時該注意的地方，告訴你讓信件脫穎而出的小祕訣。

 小建議大思考 Suggestions

#WowFactor

　　曾經有學者做研究，從你收到詢問信開始計算，回覆時間拉得越長，其效益將以驚人的速率下降到冰點。研究數據固然只是一個參考值，但是「迅速回覆」在現今網路資訊流通快速的世界的確扮演重要角色。客戶不僅有

3 #魔鬼藏在細節裡

#CanIPickUpYourBrain #DorieClark

　　就像杜克大學的教授 Dorie Clark，同時也是多本暢銷書作家及行銷策略顧問說的 "Can I pick your brain?（我可以請教一下嗎？）" 這句話已經被過度使用到讓人覺得隨便且欠缺考慮；"**I would like to have your advice.（我想要徵求您的意見。）**" 則會是一個更為有誠意並且明確銜接下文的請求，對方可以很快明白你找他的「原因」及「動機」。換句話說，這封信的目的不單純只是「借我問一下」，而應該看成與專業人士建立人脈關係。

書中用「**#hashtag**」標註的名人觀點，提供你在動筆前更多元的思考方向，創造更多讓自己勝出的機會。

4 寫作步驟示範

依單元情境整理出「起」、「承」、「轉」、「合」書寫步驟，帶你思考開頭該如何下筆、段落該如何發展。按部就班掌握重點原則，適切傳達感受與需求，寫一封有溫度的英文書信。

書信寫作步驟 Step by Step

STEP 1 提升你與對方的「連結性」

It's a pleasure to **make your acquaintance**. It was really nice to chat about your new campaign at annual meeting last month.

上個月很高興能與您在年度會議上結識，並且有機會了解您的新專案。

5 情境與範例

各單元都有符合真實情況的**情境故事**，帶你身歷其境進行寫作演練，並按照前面提示的寫作步驟，提供完整的**書信範例**。

情 境 Situation

年關將近，身為公司新人的你，被分派負責公司旗下主題公園的周年慶活動，你尋覓了幾家傢俱公司的手工藝品項目，希望能得到快速回覆，讓你獲得充足的資訊可以呈報上級……

範 例 Example

To Whom It May Concern:

6 實用例句

依單元情境列出**常用例句範例**，請反覆練習並加以熟記。需要書寫時，便能依個人需求套入文章。

實用例句應用指南

❶ I hate to bother you about this again.
很不想為此再次打擾你。

❷ **I was wondering if** we could have your review by Friday?
我想知道，星期五之前是否能收到您的回饋呢？

❸ **It would be very helpful if you could** complete/finish/do this by [date and time].

7 單字片語

單字片語應用指南

❶ **illustrated** 配有精美插圖的
▶ The **illustrated** storybook I bought for my nephew has become his one of his favorites.
我買給我姪子附有精美插圖的故事書已經成為他最喜歡的東西之一了。

❷ **prompt** （動詞）促使某人決定／去做某件事情
"prompt someone to do something"
▶ What **prompted** you to sell your company?
是什麼讓你決定要賣了你的公司？

貼心補充好用的單字、片語、慣用語及句型，並加上實用例句，帶你熟悉相關用法，增進寫作字彙量。

記得飛鴿傳書（**pigeon post**）的年代嗎？

誰記得啦！

但是可以稍微想像吧？如果此刻的我們穿越到那個年代，我們對於「怎麼還沒回我」的等待期將會多麼煎熬、崩潰、覺得厭世。幾千年來，人類試圖改進聯繫彼此的方式，科技的無遠弗屆體現在溝通的即時性上，我們不僅可以透過各種有趣方便的軟體聯繫對方，而且僅需要不到一秒鐘的時間，訊息就已經跨越海洋飛到對方的手機裡。不過，也正因為文字訊息頻繁地在商務人士或是親朋好友的收信匣之間往來，海量的訊息幾乎是大家的收件匣常態，「被看見」反而更具有挑戰性了。有多少人的 LINE 或 Email 的未讀信件高達上百、上千封呢？你所寄出的訊息是否也在那「未讀」的行列之中，或是更令人覺得被忽視的「已讀不回（**left on read**）」呢？

換句話說，即使科技的進步拉近我們與世界任何角落的距離，人與人之間的「溝通」依然存在令人玩味的訣竅，這些訣竅可以說是語言的藝術、遣詞用字甚至是「話術」等等，從「怎麼寫」到面對面之後的「如何說」，都需要我們在表達自我前用心斟酌的「片刻」。這個片刻裡，我們揣摩對方的心情，我們檢視自己的文字是否表達清晰，避免造成誤會，我們更進一步希望這些文字能夠達成特訂的目的，這個片刻真的不容易。

這本書要獻給在「怎麼寫」的各種情境裡感到遲疑、總是擔心是否可以按下傳送鍵的你，為你提供策略與建議，以及適用於各種情境的參考範例，和許多好用的例句與單字、片語，希望你能從中擷取需要的用法，寫出一封封能確實傳達需求的訊息。

你寄出的信息，就是你的門面，是對方認識你、了解你的目的，也是進一步與你達成共識的途徑。也因為有著單向溝通的先天阻礙，更需要你在那「片刻」裡儘可能的考量到你所能發揮的語言資源，才能帶著自信按下傳送鍵，然後幸運的話，或許不到一分鐘的時間，無聲卻有效積極的溝通橋樑，送回了你需要的回覆。

祝福你。

娜娜 2019.6.21 板橋

目錄

Part 2 THANK YOU 謝謝

商務篇 BUSINESS

熟人篇 FRIENDS

目錄

Part 3 SORRY 對不起

商務篇 BUSINESS

熟人篇 FRIENDS

Part 1

PLEASE 請

好禮貌運動
關於「請」在商務、熟人間的大哉問

商務篇 BUSINESS

 # 熟人篇 FRIENDS

When a Client Ignores You or Disappears into Thin Air...

當客戶忽略你或消失時……

當潛在客戶不讀不回你的訊息郵件，想放棄了嗎？先試試看本帖提供的不同方案、策略，再決定要不要放棄吧。

小建議大思考 Suggestions

雖然我們很難去臆測對方之所以不回覆的確切原因，排除對方可能是被外星人綁架所以人間蒸發之外，客戶不回覆大概會是以下幾種：

❶ 找到比你更好（可能更便宜、更親切、更順眼等等）的選項，回信拒絕你不僅尷尬又多此一舉，不如已讀不回。

❷ 還沒那麼急迫要決定，所以擱置也懶得回覆。

❸ （暫時）沒有需求。

❹ 手邊有一百萬件事情要處理，還沒輪到你這一件。

#theMagicEmail #BlairEnns

加拿大銷售策略專家 Blair Enns 在他的網站 Win Without Pitching 上提倡要把「培養客戶」當成銷售過程中重要的關鍵，即使看不見立即的回報，也要找到方式維繫客戶關係。當客戶不再回你訊息，不如把情緒字眼抽掉，中性大方的直言：

▶ "I haven't heard from you on [project/opportunity] so I'm going to assume you've gone in a different direction or your priorities have changed."

既然我們商談的 [專案／合作機會] 遲遲沒有下文,我猜想您或許已有別的選項或是決定。

以上這樣的方式比較適合「已經有信件往返關係,也討論到合作可能性跟其他細節,但從某封你寄出的郵件後,隔了十個工作天以上卻沒有再收到回音」的情境。如果你是寄出第一封陌生拜訪信件沒有回音,想要繼續出擊,請參考「請」篇的 LETTER 6：〈The Art of Following Up Without Being Annoying 詢問後續發展(合作可能)又不惹人厭的藝術〉。

 書信寫作步驟 Step by Step

方案 A（Blair Enns 的 "Magic Email" 模板）

STEP 1　直言[1]

I haven't heard from you on [project/opportunity] so I'm going to assume you've gone in a different direction or your priorities have changed.

既然我們商談的 [專案／合作機會] 遲遲沒有下文,我猜想您或許已有別的選項或是決定。

STEP 2　大方提供未來協助

Let me know if we can be of assistance in the future.

如果未來有需要我們提供協助的地方,請告訴我。

---

[1] 來源：https://www.winwithoutpitching.com/magic-email/

方案 B

STEP 1　溫和委婉的點出沒有下文的事實

Knowing that you must be very busy with the Art Festival. I hope you don't mind If I float this back to the top of your inbox.

知道您必定因藝術節而十分忙碌，希望您不介意我將這封信又浮出至您的信箱頂端。

STEP 2　開新的話題以利展望未來

I see a great opportunity for your project to increase traffic to your website, add extras to your services, and boost your profits. If things change and you are interested in our services, we are pleased to help you achieve these goals.

我能預見這個合作將為您的網站帶來更大流量，為您的服務增色，並且提升您的獲利。如果情況有變動而您仍然對我們的服務有興趣，我們很樂意協助您達成這些目標。

 情 境 Situation

上個月你跟一位潛在客戶透過郵件聯繫上，經歷幾次信件往返，感覺有發展合作可能，沒想到，兩個禮拜以來卻再也沒有收到對方的回信，你想要再度聯繫對方，但是不知道該怎麼做……

範 例 Example

Dear Miss Smith,

We haven't heard from you on the web design project. At this point, we have to assume that you've gone in a different direction or your priorities have changed.

Based on what we discussed before, we have drawn up three strategies to increase traffic to your website, add extras to your services and boost your profits. If things change, we are pleased to help you achieve these goals.

Sincerely,
Serena

親愛的 Smith 小姐,

由於我們商談的網頁設計的合作案遲遲沒有下文,我們猜想您方或許已經有別的選項或是決定。

根據先前的溝通過程,我們研擬了三大策略來為您的網站帶來更多的流量,為您的服務增色,並提升您的獲利。如果情況有變動而您仍然有興趣合作,我們很樂意協助您達成這些目標。

誠摯地,
Serena

實用例句應用指南

❶ I know how busy you must be managing your team during high season. Would it be better if I give you a call?
我知道正值旅遊旺季,您一定疲於經營團隊事務。不知道如果我撥電話給您會不會比較方便呢?

❷ I hope the information I shared with you about web design was helpful.

我希望先前分享給您參考的網站資訊對您有幫助。

---

❸ We were wondering whether this project is still a priority for your team. Since this is time-sensitive, we would like to let you know that we are ready to assist you.

不知道這個案子是否還是您手邊優先代辦的事項，因為這是有時效性的，我們想告訴您，我們隨時準備好要協助您。

---

❹ **If we can be of any assistance**, please, feel free to contact us.

如果有我們能協助的地方，請隨時聯繫我們。

---

❺ Your website reminds me of a past client: Yum Yum Company and we successfully helped them drive traffic to their website in two days.

您的網站讓我想到我們的一位客戶：好美味公司，我們成功的幫助他們在兩天內提升網站流量。

---

❻ The video [Link] about how customers can interact with each other using social media could be relevant to the project you are working on. Let me know if you find this helpful.

這個關於消費者如何透過使用社群媒體來交流的影片 [連結] 跟您正在處理的專案很有關聯，讓我知道您是否覺得有幫助到您。

慣用語與句型應用指南

disappear/vanish into thin air （查無原因）消失得無影無蹤

▶ It was almost as if she had **vanished into thin air**.

她就好像憑空消失了。

單字片語應用指南

❶ high season / peak season　旅遊旺季

▶ Tickets are much more expensive during **high season**.
旅遊旺季時的票券都會變得貴很多。

★ ↔ **low season** 旅遊淡季

❷ time-sensitive　有時效性的

▶ **time-sensitive** documents
有效期的文件

❸ traffic　網路流量

▶ We can give you advice on how to increase your website **traffic**.
我們能提供您關於如何促進網站流量的建議。

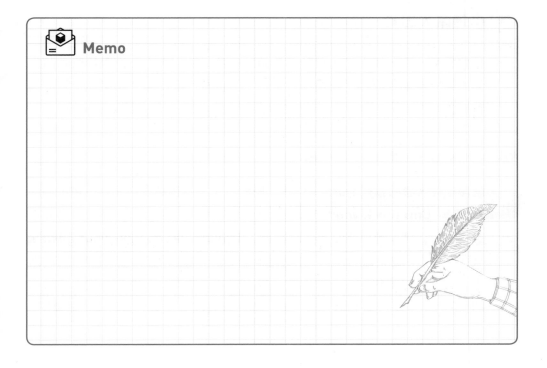

Memo

LETTER ❷

The Right Way to Ask for Someone's Help

正確請求幫助的問法

活在有 Google 的時代，當我們遇到疑難雜症想請教各方高手，只要在鍵盤上敲打關鍵字立即可以得到回應。不過，若我們期盼特定的對象能針對我們手邊的事務，提供更好的意見，這就變得不容易了。若不希望你的請求信件石沈大海，你得花一點心思。這封信的亮點是「互相幫助（two-way street）」，除了詢問對方，記得也要尊重對方的時間與精神。

 小建議大思考 Suggestions

換位思考一下，如果你是在某專業領域相當成功的人士，你對於收到陌生人寄來一封郵件問你「欸借問一下……」會有什麼反應？如果你不想成為那個讓對方可能想翻白眼的「冒失鬼」，請在寫信之前做好準備。

#CanIPickUpYourBrain #DorieClark

就像杜克大學的教授 Dorie Clark，同時也是多本暢銷書作家及行銷策略顧問說的 "Can I pick your brain?（我可以請教一下嗎？）" 這句話已經被過度使用到讓人覺得隨便並欠缺考慮；**"I would like to have your advice.（我想要徵求您的意見。）"** 則會是一個更為有誠意並且明確銜接下文的請求，對方可以很快明白你找他的「原因」及「動機」。換句話說，這封信的目的不單純只是「借我問一下」，而應該看成與專業人士建立人脈關係。

❶ 尋找共通點，花點時間了解對方的背景，可以帶入信息裡面，帶給對方驚喜。

❷ 既然是互惠，你能為對方帶來什麼？你可以怎麼介紹你自己，讓對方覺得回應你的問題，也能從你身上得到意想不到的正面價值？

#RelationshipBuilding #SallieKrawcheck

被稱作華爾街女王的 Sallie Krawcheck 曾說過，與小她好幾輪的年輕夥伴建立關係讓她的人際網路更多元豐富。所以想想你正在做的是什麼？有什麼重要性？你的專業可以提供什麼協助？可以同時讓你的「請求」更加吸睛、具體化，並達到互助的效果。

 書信寫作步驟 Step by Step

STEP 1　提升你與對方的「連結性」

It's a pleasure to **make your acquaintance**. It was really nice to chat about your new campaign at the annual meeting last month.
上個月很高興能與您在年度會議上結識，並且有機會了解您的新專案。

STEP 2　清楚表達需要對方幫什麼忙（會請對方而不是找其他人的「原因」）

❶ Our client [name] and my team work together on A project, and we are informed that you are not only an experienced but a talented B2C[1] marketer. We were wondering maybe you could spare some time to provide some input.
我們的客戶 [名字] 正在跟我的團隊一起進行 A 計畫，我們得知您不僅對 B2C 非常有經驗並且具有專才，我們在想能不能請您撥冗提供我們一點建議。

---

[1] B2C：Business to Customers 企業對消費者的電子商務模式

❷ Or would you be willing to answer a few questions via email?

或者您願意透過電子郵件回答我們幾個問題呢？

STEP 3　禮貌結語，同時讓對方有台階下

❶ Thank you so much for considering my request.

謝謝您花時間考慮我的請求。

---

❷ Knowing that it's been a busy week for your department, if you don't have time, could you recommend someone else for us to speak to?

知道您的部門這一週相當忙碌，如果您實在抽不開身，您是否可以為我們推薦其他人？

情 境 Situation

你負責的專案遇到困難，想要向資深主管尋求一點建議，雖然是同一間公司，不過你與這位經理只有一面之緣，你很希望對方在百忙之中樂於提供協助……

Dear Mr. Jonson,

I am Serena from marketing department. Our client Peter and our team work on Plus project, expected to draw over 3000 viewers to our website per month. After reading your advice on B2C marketing campaigns last year, we believe you are the right person to ask for opinions. We were wondering if you would like to give us some advice as well.

I'd love to buy you a cup of coffee so I can share more with you about this project designed to position our company as premium brand in an increasingly competitive market. Alternatively, would you be willing to answer a few questions via email if that is more convenient for you?

Thank you for considering my request. Knowing that it's been a busy week for you working on the merging case, if you can't make it, I totally can understand.

Sincerely,
Serena

親愛的 Jonson 先生,

我是行銷部門的 Serena,我們的客戶 Peter 正在跟我的團隊一起進行 Plus 計畫,預期可以每月擴增三千名觀眾到我們網站,在閱讀過您去年針對 B2C 行銷專案的建議之後,我們相信您是能夠給予我們寶貴意見的人,我們在想或許您也有意願給我們一些建議。

想請您喝杯咖啡，我好能跟您介紹這個將為我們公司在競爭激烈的市場上建立一個優質品牌定位的重要專案，或者，您比較方便用郵件方式討論呢？

謝謝您考慮我的請求，我知道這週您也同時在忙併購案，如果您抽不開身，我也能理解。

誠摯地，
Serena

實用例句應用指南

❶ It was great meeting you at Taipei Book Fair on January 15th. I had a great time chatting with you about marketing strategies.
很榮幸與您於 1 月 15 日時在台北書展上認識，與您談論行銷策略非常愉快。

❷ I've been a fan of your website for a long time and I found your life hacks are amazingly useful and inspiring. I'd love to buy you a cup of coffee sometime and tell you how thankful I am.
我是您網站上長久以來的粉絲，我發現您的生活妙招非常啟發人心並且對我有幫助，我很希望有機會能請您喝杯咖啡，向您表達我有多感激。

❸ Your company is the exact kind of place I'd like to work at one day. Would you give me some advice on **breaking into the industry**? **It would be tremendously valuable to me**.
您的公司就是我夢想能任職的地方，有沒有可能請您提供我任何可以有機會涉入這個產業的建議？無論什麼建議對我都會非常有價值。

❹ I was hoping you would be willing to provide insights from your experience.
我希望您願意就您的經驗提供我們一點指教。

❺ I was wondering if you would like to discuss some solutions we have come up with and see if they're going astray.

我在想您是否願意與我討論一下我們目前有的幾個解決方案，然後看看是否方向正確。

❻ We wanted to reach out to tell you how much we admire your work and you are naturally the most qualified person for us to **turn to**.

我們想要聯繫並告訴您我們十分欣賞您的作品，而您自然是可以幫助我們的最有資格的人選。

❼ I'd be very grateful if you could...

我會非常的感激，如果您能……

❽ I'm writing to ask for your help... **could you, by any chance,**...?

我想請你幫個忙，你有沒有可能……？

❾ Could I ask you to do me a favor/help me with...?

能請你幫我……？

❿ I was wondering if you would mind helping me...

我在想你不知道願不願意幫我……。

⓫ **If your hands are tied**, I can totally understand.

如果你不能幫忙，我完全可以理解。

慣用語與句型應用指南

❶ Someone's hands are tied 受到限制

▶ I'd like to help you, but my **hands are tied**.
我想幫你忙，但是我身不由己。

❷ break into something 突然開始；進入

▶ She **broke into** tears.
她突然開始大哭。

▶ She really wants to **break into** show business.
她真的很想進入影視圈。

❸ make someone's acquaintance　初次相識

▶ I first **made** her **acquaintance** last month at Christina's birthday party.
我是在 Christina 的生日派對上初次認識她。

❹ turn to someone　請求幫助

▶ It's frustrating when you face difficulties and have no one to **turn to**.
遇到困難卻沒有人可以尋求幫助很令人沮喪。

單字片語應用指南

❶ acquaintance　相識的人（不是非常熟，也不能稱為朋友）

▶ He is a business **acquaintance**.
他是生意上認識的人。

❷ by any chance　（禮貌地請求／詢問）可能（嗎）；也許

▶ Would you, **by any chance**, lend me your new car for my wedding ceremony?
你有可能借我你的新車，讓我在婚禮上使用嗎？

❸ fair　（名詞）商展；博覽會

▶ career/job fair 就業博覽會

▶ new tech fair 新科技商展

▶ book fair 書展

❹ help out 幫助某人（脫離困境）；幫忙

▶ The marketing manager thanked everyone who had **helped out**.
行銷經理感謝曾經幫忙的每一個人。

💬 娜娜老師的寫作小撇步

#NeverSayNever #AdamGrant

▶ "Can I pick your brain?"
我可以請教一下嗎？（直譯：我可以拿走你的腦袋嗎？）

▶ "No, you can't pick my brain, but I will talk to you anyway."
不，你不行拿走我的腦袋，但我還是會跟你談話。

—— Adam Grant

（華頓商學院教授，心理學家，暢銷書作者）

大部分的人被問到「可以請教一下嗎？」的第一直覺反應可能會是「那我可以得到什麼？」

用成本效益分析來看待這個情況很合乎常理，卻不一定能為你的事業帶來更多「驚喜」。借用 Grant 教授的話："It's impossible to predict the utility of a meeting.（我們不可能去預測一個會面將帶給我們的效益有多大。）"

換言之，若你身為「被請教」的一方，在時間允許下不妨保持開放心情，人際網絡的連結效益常常是要拉長時間來看才會發覺的。

LETTER ③

Just a Friendly Reminder— Get Someone to Do Something

友善提醒—請某人做某事

Email 往返縱使方便，但惱人的地方就在於一封信寄出去之後像石沈大海，等不到對方的回音，而你手上的事情只能擱置，沒有進度，尤其是團隊合作過程中，總是難免遇到遲遲未收到回覆的情況。這時候除了常見的 **ASAP**（As Soon as Possible）之外，還有沒有更好的方式，善意的提醒對方並且有效提升回覆速度呢？

💬 小建議大思考 Suggestions

大家都很忙，你寄出的這封信是不只是跟對方收件匣裡上百封信件競爭，還得跟各種通訊軟體搶奪注意力，若想表達尊重對方的忙碌與時間，就必須把你這封催促回覆的信件「寫清楚」。

❶ 善用「主旨」

把截止日期放在主旨欄位

▶ Please respond by EOD Wednesday.
請在週三前回覆。

❷ 把複雜的事項條列式

▶ Here's a recap of what we discussed:
- [title] document (due: Friday 2/5)
- [title] analysis (due: Wednesday 2/10)
- [title] reviews (due: Friday 2/12)

以下是我們討論事項的概要：

- [名稱] 文件（截止日：2 月 5 日星期五）

- [名稱] 分析（截止日：2 月 10 日星期三）

- [名稱] 檢討（截止日：2 月 12 日星期五）

❸ 文末不忘提醒

▶ Your prompt response/reply would be greatly appreciated.

希望您能即時回覆，感謝您。

 書信寫作步驟 Step by Step

STEP 1　委婉說明或是幽默暗示（試情況而定）

▶ **Just to remind you that** we're still missing/awaiting your feedback.

只是提醒您，我們還缺／等您的回饋意見。

▶ I'm sorry for clogging up your inbox.

很抱歉堵塞您的信箱。

STEP 2　清楚說明你需要對方回覆的內容

❶ Here's what we still need from you:
a. Your feedback on the project
b. Your suggestions on the questionnaire

以下是我們等待您提供的：
a. 您對於專案的意見回饋
b. 您對於問卷的建議

❷ I am integrating your feedback into our team's solution proposal and will send it to the client tomorrow.

我正在把你們大家的意見回饋整合進團隊的提案裡，然後明天會寄給客戶。

STEP 3　將時間及催促原因強調清楚

I apologize for the urgency, but your opinions on this project are critical and we are looking forward to it. Could you please send me your feedback by EOD Wednesday?

對於催促您趕到抱歉，您的意見對於這個專案相當重要，我們非常期待。能請您於星期三以前將意見回饋提供給我嗎？

 情 境 Situation

你是一個人資專員，幾天前寄出了新的問卷量表給各部門的主管，眼看預定好的回覆截止日在即，卻還有好多人沒有回覆，你必須再寄一封信提醒大家⋯⋯

 範 例 Example

Dear Project Plus Team Member,

Just to remind you that we're still missing your feedback on our updated questionnaire. We value your feedback and need it as soon as possible so we can move on to the next phase. We would appreciate it if you could send it to us by noon tomorrow.

If you are having trouble with it, we would be happy to help answer questions you may have.

Sincerely,
Serena

親愛的 Plus 計畫團隊成員，

想要提醒您，目前還缺少您對於最新問卷的意見回饋，我們看重您的意見也急需收到回覆才能繼續下一階段的程序。若您能於明天中午之前回覆給我們，不勝感激。

如果您對此有任何問題，我們很樂意協助您。

誠摯地，
Serena

實用例句應用指南

❶ I hate to bother you about this again.
很不想為此再次打擾你。

❷ **I was wondering if** we could have your review by Friday?
我想知道，星期五之前是否能收到您的回饋呢？

❸ **It would be very helpful if you could** complete/finish/do this by [date and time].
如果你能在 [日期和時間] 內完成就太好了。

❹ If I don't hear from you by the end of the day, I would send it out without your feedback.
如果我今天下班前沒有得到你的回覆，我會把目前收集到的直接寄出。

❺ **We would be very grateful if** you could complete and return the questionnaire by/before November 15th 2019.
我們會很感謝，如果您能在 2019 年 11 月 15 日以前完成並且回覆這份問卷。

❻ The project is our priority. **Could you possibly** have it done by [date and time]?
這是我們目前最首要處理的計畫，您能夠在 [日期和時間] 之前完成嗎？

❼ **Would it be feasible for you to** review the proposal and send us comments by [date and time]?
如果是在 [日期和時間] 之前，您方便看一下提案內容，然後給我們意見嗎？

❽ **Would you mind** prioritizing this case over other projects?
你介意把這個專案排在優先位置嗎？

❾ Our goal is to finalize the proposal by the end of the month. Could you give me the customer analysis by noon tomorrow?
我們的目標就是在這個月底以前完成這個提案，你能在明天中午以前把顧客分析給我嗎？

單字片語應用指南

❶ by [time]　不要遲於 [時間]；在 [時間] 前

▶ I have promised her to finish this **by** two o'clock.
我已經答應她要在兩點鐘以前完成這件事情。

▶ My university application has to be submitted **by** January 1st.
我的大學申請表必須在 1 月 1 日之前繳交。

❷ clog up　（使）阻塞；堵塞

▶ Leaves are **clogging up** our gutters.
樹葉塞住我們的排水溝。

比喻信箱被「塞」滿了：

▶ Don't send out unnecessary emails that simply **clog up** someone's inbox.
不要寄一些非必要的郵件，堵塞別人的信箱。

❸ EOD （**end of day**）今天以前

注意此為商務方面的用法，在不同領域則代表不同的意思，例如：

▶ 軍事：Explosive Ordnance Disposal 爆裂物處理

▶ 電腦：end of data 資料結束

▶ 口語：end of discussion 討論結束；到此為止

❹ feasible 可行的；做得到的

▶ I don't think this project is **feasible**.
我不認為這個計畫是可行的。

❺ recap/recapitulate （重述）摘要說明

▶ To **recapitulate** what was discussed earlier, we need to improve the system.
概括一下先前討論的內容，我們需要改進系統。

❻ relatively 相較之下

▶ The tasks here are **relatively** easy for rookies.
這些任務對於新手來說相對容易。

Letters of Inquiry
詢問服務的信件

當我們去信某公司詢問服務,要求提供目錄報價或是樣品參考等等,以潛在客戶的立場,這封信寫起來比較沒有壓力,不過仍然有些狀況可以留意,例如說你希望對方能趕在某個時間點前回覆你,讓你有效地達成工作目標。本帖提供簡單又實用的例句來表達你的詢問需求,只需要簡單兩個步驟即可完成草稿。

🗨 小建議大思考 Suggestions

---

❶ 錯誤的問題不會帶來正確的資訊

詢問信件目的就在獲得你需要的確切資訊,以「精簡有效」為原則,避免用字拖泥帶水、含糊不清,造成信件往來費時又增添誤會。

❷ 禮貌永遠是不會過季的流行配件

正式有禮貌的詢問信件也會展現你的專業度,例如信件抬頭,寫"**To whom it may concern**(敬啟者)"沒有什麼問題,不過若有辦法確認聯絡窗口,當然會比起沒有特別署名收件者的信件要更有溝通效果。

 書信寫作步驟 Step by Step

STEP 1 開門見山有三種

❶ 直接請問

I am writing to inquire about your advertisement in

Modern Furniture and could you please send us your latest catalog?

我想詢問您們在《現代傢俱》上面刊登的廣告，能請您提供貴公司最新的產品目錄嗎？

❷ 委婉取向

Would it be possible for us to have some samples before we order?

在我們下單之前，是否有可能請您提供一些樣品作為參考用呢？

❸ 關於自己

We operate two theme parks in Taiwan and are looking for hand-crafted products to be our gifts to clients. Please send us your latest catalog and price lists.

我們在台灣有兩座主題公園，我們正在尋覓手工藝品來當作顧客的禮物，請提供貴公司的產品目錄及價目表。

STEP 2　畫龍點睛有三種

❶ 希望盡快回覆

It would be very helpful if you could reply as soon as possible so we could make a decision at the end of this month.

希望您能盡快回覆，我們便能在月底前做決定。

❷ 補充細節

Please, also include information about shipping and the minimum quantity for a trial order.

請同時提供運送細節以及試銷訂單的最小訂購量。

❸ 禮貌稱謝

Thank you. We are awaiting your reply.

謝謝您。我們期待您的回覆。

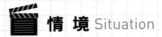
年關將近，身為公司新人的你，被分派處理年終餐會的外燴，你尋覓了幾家宴會餐飲公司，希望能得到快速回覆，讓你獲得充足的資訊可以呈報上級……

 範 例 Example

To Whom It May Concern:

I am writing to inquire about your advertisement on Facebook fan page. We are planning our year-end party and interested in "Holiday Party Package". Could you send us full details of your party services and price lists?

A prompt reply would be appreciated. We would like to make a decision at the end of this month.

Sincerely,
Serena

敬啟者：

想請問您在 Facebook 粉絲專頁的廣告內容，我們要舉辦歲末年終聯歡會，對你們「假期派對套組」有興趣。可以麻煩您提供我們宴會服務的產品細節以及價目表嗎？

麻煩請盡快回覆，我們希望在月底之前做出決定。

誠摯地，
Serena

❶ **Could** you mail us a hard copy of your catalogue and current price list?
能寄給我們紙本的產品銷售目錄以及定價表嗎？

❷ **Would it be possible** for you to send us a copy of your Winter Special brochure?
方便請您提供冬季特刊手冊給我們參考嗎？

❸ **With reference to / Regarding** your advertisement in *Modern Fabric*, we are interested in ordering your thermal fabric.
看到您在《摩登織品》上面的廣告，我們想要訂購保暖纖維。

❹ We own ten restaurants in Southern Taiwan and are planning to redecorate all of them. **Please**, send us your illustrated catalog and export price list.
我們在南台灣擁有十家餐廳，正準備要重新裝修，請提供貴公司的產品目錄以及出口價目表。

❺ **A prompt reply would be greatly appreciated**.
若您能快速回覆，不勝感激。

❻ **We look forward to hearing from you**.
我們很期待收到您的回音。

❼ **I would also like to know** on what terms you can deliver products with free shipping.
我也想知道怎樣的條件下，你們可以寄送產品不收運費。

❽ We **would be very interested in** purchasing your products if we are entitled to a volume discount.
如果能有大量訂購的折扣，我們很樂意購買你的產品。

❶ hear from someone 從某人處（透過信件、電話）得知某消息

▶ Do you **hear from** Mr. Stevenson these days?
你最近有跟史蒂文森先生聯繫嗎？

▶ We haven't **heard from** Mr. Stevenson.
我們沒有關於史蒂文森先生的消息。

▶ I am still waiting to **hear from** the bank about my mortgage.
我還在等待銀行回覆我貸款的結果。

❷ Would it be possible to...? 表達寫信者禮貌的詢問口吻

▶ **Would it be possible to** send us your color catalog by the end of this week?
能夠麻煩你在這週之前把彩色目錄寄給我們嗎？

"I would like to..." 我想要……

▶ **I would like to** know details about your catering service.
我想要知道你們外燴服務的細節。

"Would you mind..." 你能夠……嗎？

▶ **Would you mind** telephoning me during the next week?
你能夠下週找個時間用電話聯繫我嗎？

❶ illustrated 配有精美插圖的

▶ The **illustrated** storybook I bought for my nephew has become one of his favorites.
我買給我姪子附有精美插圖的故事書已經成為他最喜歡的東西之一了。

❷ prompt （動詞）促使某人決定／去做某件事情
"prompt someone to do something"

▶ Curiosity **prompted** him to ask a lot of questions.
好奇心使他問了許多問題。

（形容詞）迅速的；即時的

▶ Thank you for your **prompt** reply.
謝謝您迅速地回覆。

❸ terms （名詞）條件；條款

▶ Under the **terms** of the contract, they can have 10 percent off discount.
根據合約條款，他們可以享九折優惠。

❹ volume discount 大量購買的折扣

▶ My uncle, whose job as a clothing retailer, often gets **volume discounts** when he is purchasing.
我叔叔作為一個衣服的零售商，常常可以拿到大量購買的折扣。

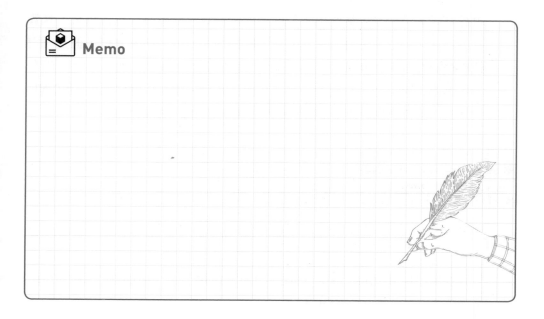

📩 Memo

Respond to Customer Inquiries
回覆客戶詢問

收到潛在客戶的詢問需求,當然是要把握機會、達成業務合作目標。不過,要怎麼回信才能讓對方滿意呢?如果對方的需求你此刻不能達成,又要怎麼委婉地告知,才能透過書面溝通建立良好形象呢?請看本帖的簡單三步驟!

 小建議大思考 Suggestions

#WowFactor

曾經有學者做研究,從你收到詢問信開始計算,回覆時間拉得越長,其效益將以驚人的速率下降到冰點。研究數據固然只是一個參考值,但是「迅速回覆」在現今網路資訊流通快速的世界的確扮演重要角色。客戶不僅有很多選擇,更可能一秒反悔,倘若想留住客戶,讓客戶對你產生 **"WOW!"** 的印象,回覆訊息的速度及高效率的溝通是必然要把握的關鍵。

 書信寫作步驟 Step by Step

STEP 1 開門道謝

We greatly appreciate your interest in our catering service.
非常感謝您對我們外燴服務的興趣。

STEP 2　告知處理方式

❶ 可以滿足要求

We have asked our sales representative in Taipei, Lucy Chang, to send you a copy of our current catalog, price list and samples.

我們已經聯繫了台北的業務代表，Lucy Chang，寄給您目前的目錄、價目清單及樣品。

❷ 無法滿足要求

Regrettably, due to an unusually large number of orders, we regret that we cannot meet your requirements. We are deeply sorry for the inconvenience.

很遺憾地，因為我們接獲大量訂單，實在無法符合您在信件中的需求。造成您的不便，我們感到很抱歉。

❸ 再次感謝或是其他服務細節

Thank you again for your interest in our products.

再次感謝您對我們的產品有興趣。

STEP 3　進一步提供幫助

If you have additional questions, please call our regional office in your area. We would be happy to meet your requirements. Attached is a list of regional offices and contact numbers.

如果您有其他問題，請聯繫我們的區域辦公室，我們竭力滿足您的需求，附件表單是我們各地區辦公室的聯繫方式。

你是 Yum Yum Catering（好美味外燴公司）的行銷業務。年關將至，你們在 Facebook 及 Instagram 所推出的各種中小型派對套餐 "Happy Meals Special" 受到中小型企業歡迎，訊息回覆量暴漲，年底之前不可能再接新訂單。今天你收到了一封詢問郵件，是一個老師想要在育幼院舉辦四十人的公益聯歡餐會，你覺得除了婉拒之外，或許可以創造更好的雙贏機會……

範 例 Example

Dear Miss Wang,

Thank you for your letter of requesting information about our Happy Meals Special posted on Facebook. We certainly appreciate your interest in our catering service.

Regrettably, due to an unusually large number of orders, we regret that we cannot meet your requirements. We are deeply sorry for the inconvenience.

However, we appreciate your kindness and we would like to propose an alternative to suit your needs. I've attached the tailored refreshments menu and price list and hope this proposal catches your fancy.

If you have further questions, just give me a call at 0800-808-808.

Yum Yum Catering serves you better.

親愛的王小姐，

謝謝您來信詢問我們在 Facebook 上公告的歡樂套餐專案，您考慮選擇我們讓我們感到很榮幸。

很遺憾地，因為我們接獲大量訂單，實在無法符合您在信件中的需求。造成您的不便，我們感到很抱歉。

然而，我們非常欣賞您的好心，因此我們提供了另外一個方案提供您參考，這樣為您量身規劃的菜單選項以及價目我也隨信件附上，看看您是否喜歡。

如果您對於我們的服務有任何問題，請直接聯繫我，連絡電話是 0800-808-808。

好美味外燴公司給您更好的服務。

實用例句應用指南

❶ Thank you very much for your inquiry.
謝謝您的詢問。

❷ **Thank you for inquiring about** our new travel plans advertised in Taipei Tourist Magazine.
謝謝您詢問我們在台北旅遊雜誌上刊登的最新旅遊方案。

❸ **In response to** your letter dated June 10th, we are pleased to send you our latest brochure and samples.
回覆您 6 月 10 日的郵件，我們很高興寄給您最新目錄以及樣品參考。

❹ We hope that the enclosed proposal and quotation/price list will suit your needs.
希望隨信附上的企劃書以及報價單／價目表能符合您的需求。

❺ **I have attached** our Winter Special brochure you requested.
附上您詢問的冬季特輯手冊。

❻ I am sharing our Winter Fantasy catalog with you.
提供您我們的「冬季夢幻」產品目錄。

❼ **The enclosed** catalog details the [feature] of our [product]
附件檔案詳細說明了我們的 [產品] 的 [特色]。

❽ If you could take a few minutes to review the enclosed information, you will find the reasons why we have been awarded the most popular travel agency in Taipei.
若您可以花點時間瀏覽一下附件檔案，您會了解我們之所以獲頒為台北最受歡迎的旅行社的原因。

❾ Please note that free-shipping service applies to Taiwan destinations only.
請留意免運服務僅適用於在台灣的運送地址。

❿ As soon as that information is available from our suppliers, our salespeople will notify you the expected delivery date.
只要我們的供應商一聯繫我們，我們的業務員便可以告訴您預計的送貨日期。

⓫ **If you have further questions**, just give me a call at [phone number] and it will be my pleasure to answer your questions.
如果您有進一步的問題，直接打 [電話號碼] 給我沒有問題，我很樂意解開您的疑問。

⓬ We hope that the information is helpful and please feel free to contact us if you have further questions about our services or the attachment.
希望這些資訊對您有幫助，如果您對於附件檔案或是我們的業務內容有任何問題，請隨時聯繫我們。

慣用語與句型應用指南

❶ catch/strike someone's fancy　**贏得對方的喜歡、興趣**

▶ Their marketing plan really **caught/struck** my **fancy**.
他們的行銷案真的很吸引我。

❷ in response to N　**回覆您的（信件、詢問、傳真等等）**

▶ I'm writing **in response to** your fax of August 12th.
茲回覆您 8 月 12 日的傳真。

response　（名詞）回覆

▶ She got a **response** to her request.
她的請求得到回覆。

❸ Please note that...　**請注意……**

▶ **Please note that** we will be closed on Monday.
請注意我們週一沒有營業。

單字片語應用指南

❶ convenience　**方便**

"at your convenience"　**意指當你方便的時候**

▶ The products you ordered will be delivered **at your convenience**.
您訂購的物品將會依照您方便的時間運送。

"at your earliest convenience"　**意指麻煩盡快**

▶ Please return the completed form **at your earliest convenience**.
請盡快將填好的表格寄回。

❷ inquiry 詢問；打聽資訊

▶ The institution now welcomes **inquiries** from prospective applicants.
該機構現在歡迎申請者來信詢問。

❸ meet/satisfy/fulfil/suit your requirements 符合（需求）

▶ Our travel plan definitely can **meet your requirements**.
我們的旅行安排一定能符合您的需求。

❹ regarding / concerning 關於

▶ I have few questions **regarding** your earlier comments.
關於你先前的評論，我有幾個問題。

❺ request （名詞）請求；要求

▶ We made/submit a **request** for a pedestrian crossing near the elementary school.
我們請求在小學附近增設人行道。

★ 搭配介係詞有 by, on, upon 等，意思是如果有提出需求的話可以提供。

▶ Tickets are available **by/on/upon request**.
如果有需要的話，票券是可以提供的。

❻ stock 庫存；存量

▶ Cowboy hats are out of **stock**.
牛仔帽子現在缺貨中。

❼ tailor 專門訂製（因應特別需求）

▶ We at YumYum Catering want your event to be the best it can possibly be, so we are happy to **tailor** our catering service to your company's specific needs.
我們好美味外燴公司致力讓您的活動精彩萬分，我們非常樂意提供客製化服務來滿足您的所有需求。

The Art of Following Up Without Being Annoying

詢問後續發展（合作可能）又不惹人厭的藝術

「追進度」是一門藝術，必須透過訊息「置入行銷」你的目的。你想要把自己的服務推銷給對方，同時也不能讓對方覺得太有壓迫感。本帖主要以潛在客戶為例，如果是求職者在面試之後主動聯絡公司方關心後續發展，請參考 PART2〈THANK YOU 謝謝篇〉的實用例句應用指南。

 小建議大思考 Suggestions

❶ 小心變成黑名單

如果你的時機抓得不好，例如間隔了太久才來噓寒問暖，不免讓人懷疑，是否自己是你的第二選擇？或是你太過「黏人」，也可能造成不容易修補的壞印象。

❷ 小心又不失溫柔地喚醒對方記憶

「提醒對方」時將禮貌態度及服務熱情合而為一，例如：「嘿，我們上次才在哪裡見過面記得嗎？」、「上次可以在發明展上面見到您真的是非常榮幸」，或「不知道您有沒有收到我們寄給您的彩色目錄了呢？」

❸ 打造吸睛的主旨

面對潛在客戶，信件主旨會影響到對方在百忙之中，是否會為此多停留一秒鐘的可能性。

例如「直接告訴對方信件裡的好康」是什麼，例如 "A special discount for Yum Yum Catering（提供好美味外燴公司特別優惠）"

或是「點出對方的需求」，像是 "Three strategies for your work productivity（提升工作效能的三個策略）"、"Five Easy Ways to Drive More Traffic to Your Website（五個簡單技巧，吸引更多人造訪您的網站）"、"How to Start Getting Traffic to Your Website（如何吸引更多人造訪您的網站）"。

 書信寫作步驟 Step by Step

STEP 1　喚醒對方的記憶

Glad we got to meet at trade show in Frankfurt last week. I appreciated having the opportunity to learn more about how we can meet your needs.

很高興我們上週在法蘭克福的商展上會面，很感謝有這個機會能了解我們如何能滿足您的需求。

STEP 2　刺激對方的需求

❶ I have been thinking about how to help you increase your website traffic and thought you might appreciate this case study on how we helped a similar company achieve their goal in three months.

我一直在思考如何能幫助您增加您網站的流量，我們有一個客戶跟您的情況很類似，我們在三個月內就達到他的預期目標。你或許有興趣參考了解一下。

❷ Since the brochure I gave you only covers general information, I was wondering whether you have some specific questions on certain issues.

因為產品手冊只有提供一般的資訊，不知道您是否有特殊的疑問並無法在手冊上面找到解答。

STEP 3　進一步提供服務

I suggest that we meet up and I would love to arrange a brief demonstration.

我提議我們可以碰個面詳談，並且我想要安排一個簡短的展示。

STEP 4　禮貌致謝

I look forward to discussing this matter further.

我期待能有更近一步的洽談。

情 境 Situation

你兩個星期前參加了一場商展，跟幾位新創公司的老闆交換了名片，其中一位特別提到他們網站每次辦活動都成效不彰，連抽獎都沒有達到預期網路瀏覽量，你當下馬上推薦你的行銷服務，兩人相談甚歡，可是卻從此沒有下文，你想要主動聯繫對方……

Subject: A marketing strategy for boosting your website traffic

Dear Mr. Janson,

Glad we got to meet at the trade show in Taipei weeks ago.

I was thinking about you mentioned that you wanted to know how to increase your website traffic and thought you might appreciate this case study on how we helped a similar company achieve their goal in two months.—[link to the case]

I would love to discuss how we can make this solution work for you. Are you free for a phone call tomorrow?

Sincerely,
Serena

信件主旨：增加網路流量的妙方

Janson 先生您好，

很高興我們幾星期前在台北商展碰面。我後來一直想到你提到想要增加你的網站瀏覽量，我們有一個客戶跟你的情況很類似，我們在兩個月內就達到他的預期目標。你或許有興趣參考了解一下 [網址連結]。

我也想要針對這個解決方案與您進一步商談，希望可以解決您的問題。請問您明天有空通電話嗎？

誠摯地，
Serena

❶ You have probably received the brochures you requested about our Winter Special product lines.
您應該已經收到我們寄給您冬季商品目錄了。

❷ **We wondered whether** you received the catalog of our summer collection and price lists.
不知道您是否已經收到我們的夏季產品的型錄跟價目表了。

❸ **Thank you for giving me the opportunity to** meet with you today. Here's the recap for our meeting.
謝謝您今天撥冗與我開會。在這邊彙整一下關於會議的幾個要點。

❹ If you could place your order today, our premium delivery will ensure you receive your items within two working days.
如果您今天就下訂，我們的尊榮遞送服務會確保您在兩個工作天內收到您的品項。

❺ We are offering your company a special discount for our thermal fabric products.
針對我們的保暖纖維商品，我們會提供貴公司特別折扣。

❻ I have checked in with my boss and we would be happy to arrange a demonstration for your company.
經與主管確認完畢，我們會滿足您提出的特殊要求。

❼ Again, it was great meeting you at the conference and I hope to see you again soon.
很高興與您在會議上再次碰面，希望很快再見面。

❽ Thank you for your consideration of my suggestions.
謝謝您考慮我們的提議。

❾ We look forward to hearing from you as soon as possible.
希望很快能有您的回音。

慣用語與句型應用指南

I suggest... 我建議……

請大家要小心，很多時候我們會直接以中文思維來寫英文句子，就變成 "I suggest you..." 但這是錯誤的文法，正確用法如下：

加 **that** 子句

▶ I **suggest that** you call him as soon as possible.
我建議你馬上打電話給他。

加 **Ving**

▶ I **suggest calling** him as soon as possible.
我建議馬上打給他。

加 **N**

▶ My boss **suggested a solution** to this problem.
我老闆針對這個問題建議了一個解決方案。

單字片語應用指南

❶ check in with someone （非正式）與某人針對某事商談

▶ I have to go to a meeting now, but I'll **check in with** you later.
我現在要去開會，但是我等一下會去找你談。

---

❷ discount 折扣

★ 常見搭配動詞

▶ The company **offer/give** customers a 5 percent **discount** when they pay in cash.
公司提供以現金結帳的消費者九五折優惠。

▶ Students **are entitled** to a **discount**.
學生可以享有折扣。

★ 常見搭配介系詞

▶ Tickets are available to students **at** a **discount**.
學生購票享優惠。

---

❸ trade show/fair　商展；展銷會

▶ Our company unveiled a new product at the annual **trade show**.
我們公司在年度商展上發布新產品。

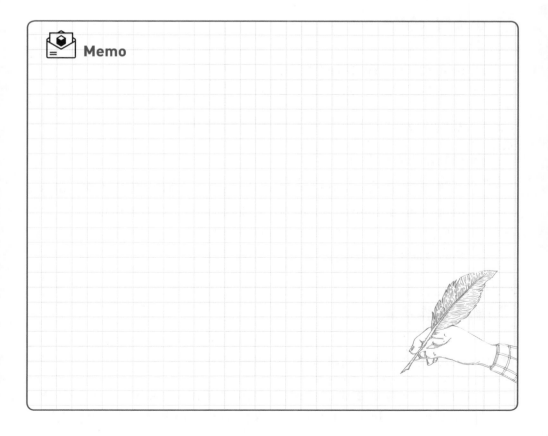

Memo

Please Forgive Me
請原諒我

不管是無意或有心，一場誤會或一次意外，我們都有可能直接或間接地傷了朋友的心，透過文字能緩和彼此之間的情緒，給予對方一點空間慢慢消化，不失為一種修補關係的方式。

💬 小提醒大領悟 Reminders

❶ 重點不是對不起這三個字

這是一個向對方打開心扉，承認自己所造成傷害的過程，「對不起（I am sorry）」三個字只是這個過程的開場白而已。

❷ 目的並非獲得原諒

「請求原諒（begging for forgiveness）」跟「真誠致歉（giving people an authentic apology）」在對方感受上是有差別的。與其想要「獲得」原諒，不如認真表達關於「意識到」自己所造成的傷害並感到後悔與抱歉，是你所能「給予」對方的誠意。

書信寫作步驟 Step by Step

STEP 1 表達歉意，意識到對方受傷的事實

I am so sorry that I overslept and ruined everything. I know by saying so doesn't even make anything better. **I should**

have been there for you.

抱歉我睡過頭搞砸了這一切，我知道現在說什麼都不會改變這個事實。我應該要在你身邊支持你（實際上我並沒有做到）。

STEP 2　告訴他你的後悔（視情況解釋事件始末）

❶ I broke my promise and I am truly sorry for what I have done.

我答應你的事情沒有做到，對於我所做的事情，我深深感到抱歉。

---

❷ I was terribly burnt out and I failed to deal with it. **To make matters worse**, I made you suffer.

我整個人一團糟，我沒把自己照顧好。更糟的是，我還害到你。

STEP 3　展現誠意，強調下不為例

I totally understand why you don't want to talk to me and it's all my fault. If you let me, I would do anything to make it up to you.

我理解你之所以完全不想跟我說話的原因，這都是我的錯。如果你給我機會，我會盡一切努力來補償你。

🎬 情 境 Situation

你答應朋友 Daniela 要擔任她論文研究焦點訪談的紀錄人，參與訪談的對象來自各個學校的教授，能夠把大家約在一起，相當不容易。Daniela 幾天前還特地提醒你訪談地點與時間，沒想到，你因為忙於自己的專案截止日，已經連續好幾天沒有睡覺，訪談這一天你竟然睡過頭，醒來的時候已經來不及趕往現場。你看著手機裡面好幾通未接來電以及留言，你很氣自己，明明調了好幾個鬧鐘，怎麼還變成這樣？你撥了電話給 Daniela，卻直接轉進語音信箱，你到底該怎麼向 Daniela 解釋？

Hi Daniela,

I am so sorry that I overslept and ruined everything. I know by saying so doesn't even make anything better. I made a promise but I didn't deliver. **I can't apologize enough for being such a terrible friend**.

You were there for me when no one else was, but I let you down. I don't mean to make excuses, but I have been staying up late for weeks to meet deadlines. I did set many alarms last night but none of them woke me up. I am really sorry that I **messed up.**

I won't ask for your forgiveness now. **It's your call** and I will fully respect that. I just want to say if you let me, I would do anything to make it up to you.

Take Care,
Serena

嗨 Daniela，

抱歉我睡過頭搞砸了這一切，我知道現在說什麼都不會改變這個事實。我答應你要幫忙，卻沒做到。我對你真的非常的抱歉，抱歉我是一個如此糟糕的朋友。

你曾經在沒有人支持我的時候陪著我，但是我卻讓你失望了。我不是故意要找藉口，是我已經好幾天為了趕截止日熬夜沒有睡覺，我昨天晚上也設了好幾個鬧鐘，但是卻沒有一個叫醒我，我真的非常抱歉我搞砸了。

我不是要求你的原諒，決定權在你，我會完全尊重你。

我只想跟你說，如果你給我機會，我會盡一切努力來補償你。

保重，
Serena

實用例句應用指南

❶ I know I **crossed the line** and I am so sorry that I hurt you so much.

我知道我越界了，真的很對不起，我傷你那麼深。

❷ So sorry that I failed you. **I can't apologize enough for being such a terrible friend**.

我對你真的非常抱歉，抱歉我是一個如此糟糕的朋友。

❸ **You were there for me** when no one else was, but I **let you down**.

你曾經在沒有人支持我的時候陪著我，但是我卻讓你失望了。

❹ I am sorry that you had to put up with this. **You deserve better**.

我很抱歉你必須忍受這些，你值得更好的對待。

❺ I have been acting selfishly and my behavior is causing you great stress.

我一直都好自私，造成你很大的壓力。

❻ I am deeply sorry for lying to my best friend.

我很抱歉欺騙我最好的朋友。

❼ I took those who love me for granted. **I was downright selfish**.

我把那些愛我的人當成理所當然。我真的是太自私了。

❽ I regret not telling you the truth.
我後悔沒有對你說實話。

❾ I am sincerely sorry for putting you through my terrible behavior.
我真的很抱歉讓你經歷我可怕的行為。

❿ **I have come to realize** how much I have hurt those people I love so much by shutting them out of my life, especially you.
我開始了解到我是如何傷害我身邊我所愛的人們，把他們拒於門外，尤其是你。

⓫ If you want me out of your life, I will understand.
如果你想要我滾出你的生活，我完全理解。

⓬ I won't ask for your forgiveness now. **It's your call** and I will fully respect that.
我不會要求你現在的原諒，決定權在你，我也會尊重。

慣用語與句型應用指南

❶ cross the line   踩到底線；當你做了某些行為，讓對方覺得無法接受

▶ The magazine **crossed the line** when they published topless pictures of the Duchess of Cambridge.
這家雜誌刊出劍橋公爵夫人裸照，真的是太過分了。

❷ I should have p.p.
惋惜、懊悔「原本應該」要做到，但是真實情況並沒有做到。

▶ I **should have told** you the truth. I am sorry.
我早應該要告訴你真相的，我很抱歉。

▶ You **should have come** to the party last night. We had fun.
你昨天晚上應該要來派對的，我們玩得很開心。

❸ make matters worse　讓事情更糟

▶ If you are not aware of the situation, just stop talking so you don't **make matters worse**.
如果你不知道情況的話，你就不要再講話讓事情更糟了。

❹ mess up　搞砸；弄糟

▶ Breaking up with the one of your life could really **mess your** life up.
跟一生摯愛分手會讓你的生活頓時變得一團糟。

單字片語應用指南

❶ call　（非正式用法）抉擇；決定

▶ It's truly a tough **call** and no one can tell you what to do.
這真的很難決定，而且也沒有人可以告訴你要怎麼做。

▶ It should be your **call** because it's your plan.
這應該由你來決定，因為這是你的計畫。

❷ downright　（尤其表示負面的）非常；極端的

▶ I still don't understand why you are **downright** rude and obstructive.
我真的不懂為什麼你一定要如此粗魯無禮、處處與人作對。

❸ fail　辜負；未能達成、做到對方期待的情況

▶ I **failed** my girlfriend in her moment of need.
在我女朋友最需要我的時候，我辜負了她。

❹ make excuses　找藉口編理由

▶ I am done with your lies. Stop **making excuses**.
我受夠你的謊言了。不要再編藉口了。

❺ make up for something 彌補；補償

▶ You can never **make up for** what you have done to me.
你對我所做的一切，你永遠都無法彌補。

❻ put up with something/someone 忍耐；忍受

▶ I can't **put up with** his bad temper.
我無法忍受他的壞脾氣。

❼ put someone through something
讓（某人）經歷（不愉快的事情）

▶ I am sorry that I **put you through** this.
我很抱歉我讓你經歷這些。

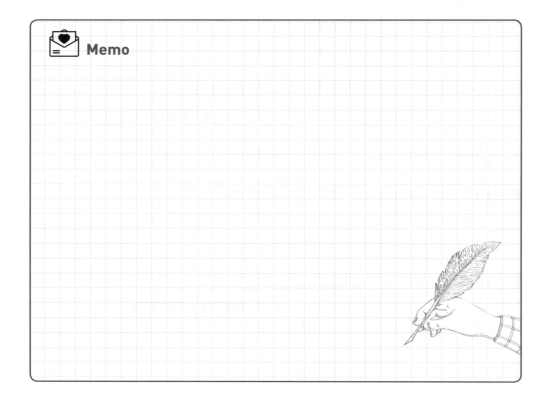

💌 **Memo**

LETTER ⑧

Ask for a Letter of Recommendation
請求幫忙寫推薦信

找人寫推薦信的這個「請求」時常讓大家感到頭痛，不管是學校的教授或是工作上主管，即使彼此認識，提出這個請求時難免感到緊張，害怕會被對方拒絕。參考本帖的建議與撰寫策略，幫自己打造一封得體又能達成目的的請求信。

 小提醒大領悟 Reminders

#WatchtheTime

預留多一點時間給對方是必要也是禮貌。一般來說，以申請的截止日往前推算一到兩個月，都是合理範圍；假設對方遲遲沒有回音，也可以趕緊考慮其他人選。不過，這並不意味著你可以漫天撒網的同時向許多人請求推薦信，世界很小，小心讓對方誤會你沒有誠意。

 書信寫作步驟 Step by Step

STEP 1　說明來信目的，禮貌詢問對方的意願

It's been a while since we discussed my career plan and I finally decided to study abroad. I was wondering if you would be willing to write a recommendation letter for me.

距上次與您討論我的職涯計畫已經隔了好一陣子了，我終於要準備出國讀書，不知道您願不願意幫我寫推薦信。

STEP 2　說明為什麼你選擇對方作為推薦人

Thanks to your guidance, I have greatly benefited from your marketing class. I felt inspired and decided to work in marketing industry.

感謝您的指導，我從您的行銷課程中獲益良多，啟發了我作下投身行銷產業的決定。

STEP 3　細節補充（提供你的經歷，及對方該如何寄送已經完成的推薦信）

I've attached my resume and cover letter to refresh your memory of my achievements in college.

我有附上我的簡歷讓您回顧一下我在大學達成的事蹟。

STEP 4　感謝對方／給對方台階下

Thank you for considering my request and being such a great mentor.

謝謝您考慮我的請求，謝謝您是一位如此棒的導師。

 **情 境** Situation

大學畢業後，你在行銷工作崗位做了兩年，最近決定要出國唸書，你想請大學時期一直很鼓勵你追求夢想的教授幫你寫推薦信……

Dear Professor Lee,

Hope this mail finds you well.

It's been a while since we discussed my career plan and I finally decided to study abroad. I was wondering if you would be willing to write a recommendation letter for me.

Thank you for spending extra time going over my research proposal and discussing my problems. If it weren't for your encouragement, I would have never realized my potential. I will always be grateful for that.

I've attached my resume and cover letter to refresh your memory of my achievements in college. The recommendation letter must be submitted online by November 25th 2019 and if you allow me, I will send you a reminder email two weeks before it's due. However, I know you must be very busy, and I would understand if you couldn't write me one. That you would take the time to read and consider my request means a lot to me.

Thank you for being such a great mentor.

Hope to hear from you soon.

Sincerely,
Serena

親愛的李教授，

希望您一切安好。

我是 Serena，距離上一次與您談論我的職涯計畫已經好久了，而我終於決定要出國唸書了，我想問您願不願意幫我寫推薦信。

謝謝您額外花時間與我討論研究計畫書以及我的問題。要不是您的鼓勵，我難以發揮自己長才。為此，我永遠感謝您。

我有附上我的簡歷讓您回顧一下我在學校達成的事蹟。申請資料必須在 2019 年 11 月 25 日截止日之前上傳，如果您允許的話，截止日兩週之前我會提醒您。然而，我知道您非常忙碌，如果您不能幫我寫推薦信，我也能理解。謝謝您花時間閱讀這封信並且考量我的請求。

謝謝您，您是一位非常棒的導師。

希望很快聽到您的回音。

誠摯地，
Serena

實用例句應用指南

❶ My name is [name] and I took your [class/seminar/ workshop] last semester.
我的名字是 [名字]，我上學期有修您的 [課／研討會／工作坊]。

❷ I am applying for a master program and **I would be more than grateful if you could** write me a strong letter of recommendation for my application.
我正準備要申請研究所，若您能為我寫推薦信，我會非常感激。

❸ **I was hoping that** you would help me advance my career. Would you be willing to write me a recommendation letter for my graduate school application?

希望您能協助我完成繼續深造的夢想，不知道您願不願意幫我寫一封研究所的推薦信？

❹ **If you're willing to** write me a recommendation letter, I will send you a pre-addressed, stamped envelope for your convenience.

如果您願意幫我寫推薦信的話，我會寄一份已經寫好住址跟貼上郵資的信封給您。

❺ The letter must be mailed directly from you to the graduate school and postmarked by May 4th 2019.

這封信需要由您直接寄給學校，郵戳必須在 2019 年 5 月 4 日以前。

❻ **I really appreciate the time and effort** you spent helping me.

很感激您花時間與心力來幫助我。

❼ I know you must be very busy and I would understand if you couldn't write me one.

我知道您非常忙碌，如果您不能幫我寫推薦信，我也能理解。

❽ Thank you so much for all you have done for me and taking the time to consider this request.

非常謝謝您為我所做的一切，並且花時間來考慮這個請求。

慣用語與句型應用指南

❶ I was wondering/hoping/thinking...　我在想⋯⋯

用「過去進行式」來表示禮貌。

▶ **I was wondering** whether you'd like to introduce your sister to me.
我在想你願不願意介紹你妹妹跟我認識。

❷ It has been (quite) a while　沒有指出過了多久，泛指好一陣子

▶ Hey, Lisa, **it's been a while**. How have you been?
嘿，麗莎，好久不見了，你都還好嗎？

▶ **It has been quite a while** since I saw her last time.
距離上一次我碰到她已經蠻長一段時間了。

while　（名詞）一段時間

▶ Please stay here for a **while**.
請在這邊稍待片刻。

awhile　（副詞）短暫片刻

▶ Stay **awhile** and don't worry.
稍待一下，別擔心。

▶ I read Harry Potter **awhile** every night and then go to bed.
我每天晚上都會讀哈利波特一下，然後再去睡覺。

❸ take the time　花費力氣去（做某件事）

▶ I regret that I didn't even **take the time** to say sorry to her.
我覺得很後悔，我連跟她說聲抱歉都沒有。

❶ due 到期、截止

▶ The application is **due** in early December.
申請在 12 月初截止。

❷ thanks to 幸虧；因為；由於

▶ We arrived early, **thanks to** good weather.
幸虧好天氣，我們提早到達。

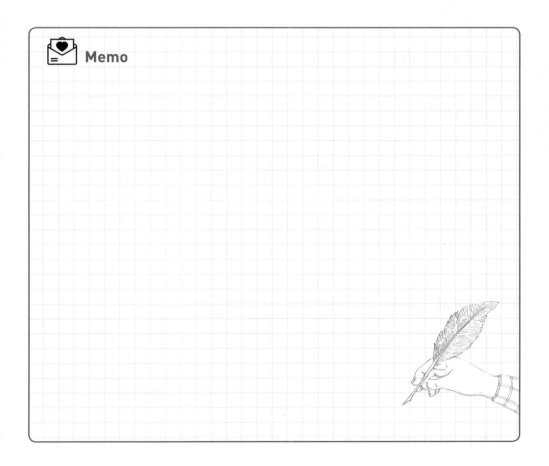

Memo

LETTER ❽ 請求幫忙寫推薦信

LETTER ❾

A Party Invitation
一張派對邀請函

生活中有好事發生想邀請朋友同樂，口頭邀約是稀鬆平常的方式，不過如果今天要一次邀請很多人，或是你在異地求學，想邀不同國籍的朋友，這種情形就很適合寄發邀請函，參考本帖的文字語句打造你自己的邀請函吧！

 小提醒大領悟 Reminders

❶ **大寫吸引目光**

為避免信件文字不夠清楚，時間、地點別忘了可以用「大寫字母」來標示，並採列點方式，都會讓訊息更清楚確實地傳達。

❷ **善用「現在進行式」**

現在進行式不是只有描述「當下發生的動作」，也可以用來表達最近的事情，本帖的舉辦活動邀請函，正可以使用這個文法句型。

書信寫作步驟 Step by Step

STEP 1 打招呼，提及活動舉辦緣由

How's life treating you? To celebrate my new life in Edinburgh, I would like to invite you to a special housewarming. Would you be interested in joining us?

最近過得如何呀？為了要慶祝我在愛丁堡的新生活，想邀請你們來參加這個特別的新居派對。有興趣嗎？

STEP 2 時間、地點、細節

❶ Date: Monday, March 22nd 2018
Time: 7 p.m.
Venue: Spring Garden, 15 Nicolson Street, Edinburgh

日期：2018 年 3 月 22 日，星期一
時間：晚上七點
地點：春天花園，尼可森街 15 號，愛丁堡

❷ My flat is right next to Tesco Express, 12 Nicolson St. It's a RED building— you can't miss it.

我的公寓在尼可森街 12 號，就在特易購快捷店旁邊。一棟紅色建築，很明顯啦！

STEP 3 其他溝通事項

❶ Call me if you get lost, [phone number]
如果你迷路的話，打 [電話號碼] 給我。

❷ Could anyone bring some puddings and drinks?
有誰可以帶甜點跟飲料過來嗎？

❸ BYOB = Bring Your Own Beer / Bring Your Own Booze
帶自己要喝的酒來。

STEP 4 溫馨呼喚

❶ Hope you can come.
希望你能來。

❷ Hope to see you there.
希望那天會見到你。

LETTER ❾ 一張派對邀請函

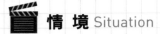
愛丁堡最近天氣出奇的好，新家附近草地櫻花盛開，你想邀請三五好友到你家享受美景、美食，這會是一個很開心的聚會，你只需要把這個想法化成文字……

範 例 Example

Hell everyone,

It's a tough winter for all of us, but hey spring is here and everything will be just fine. Does anyone fancy cherry blossoms in the Meadows?

I'm having a special housewarming on Saturday night. Would you like to come? My flat is right next to Tesco Express, 12 Nicolson St. It's a RED building– you can't miss it.

Feel free to bring anything you like and let's enjoy a lazy and cozy night.

Let me know if you can make it. I'm planning what we will do while you're here. Hope all of you can come.

Lots of love,
Serena

嗨大家好，

這個冬天對我們來說很煎熬，但是春天就來了，一切都會好轉的。想看草地上櫻花盛開的景象嗎？

週六晚上我要辦一個特別的新居派對，你們想要來嗎？我的公寓在尼可森街 12 號，就在特易購快捷店旁邊。一棟紅色建築，很明顯啦！

隨意帶你想吃的東西來，讓我們享受一個慵懶舒服的晚上吧！

讓我知道你能不能來，我正在計畫著你們來的時候我們要做些什麼，希望你們全部都能來。

很多的愛，
Serena

實用例句應用指南

❶ I hope you enjoyed your weekend/vacation.
希望你度過了美好的週末／假期。

❷ Hope you're surviving another work week.
希望你從又一個工作週活下來了。（幽默語氣）

❸ Hi, **I hope you are doing well**.
嗨，希望你一切安好呀。

❹ **I'm having a party** next Friday at my flat. So many mates from school are coming and it will be FUN.
我禮拜六要在我家辦派對。學校很多人都會來，一定會很好玩。

❺ The party will be held at The Ritz-Carlton and will be an small/informal gathering.
派對在麗池卡登飯店舉行，會是一個小型／非正式聚會。

❻ It's hard to believe it's been 10 years! With pride and joy, we invite you to join us for the Class Reunion.

不敢相信已經十年了！帶著驕傲和喜悅，我們敬邀你們參加同學會。

❼ **Please be our guest for dinner** on December 5th at seven o'clock in the evening.

請讓我們在 12 月 5 日晚上七點招待您一頓晚餐吧。

❽ What are you doing this Friday? Want to hang out at my place and watch some TV?

你這個星期五要做什麼？來我家看電視聊天如何呀？

❾ **I hope you answer "yes".**

我希望你說「好」。

❿ I am having a birthday party and it wouldn't be perfect without you guys.

我要辦生日派對，沒有你們這個派對就不完美了。

⓫ I am pretty sure that with your presence, this ordinary gathering would be extraordinary.

我相信有你的出席，這個平凡的聚會會變得不平凡。

⓬ Please RSVP as soon as you can so that I can estimate how many people will be here and what everyone will bring.

請盡快回覆確認是否可以參加，我才可以預估人數跟統計一下大家會帶什麼吃的。

⓭ **Please do let me know** whether you can join us or not.

請一定要讓我知道你是否能來參加。

⓮ In case that you wouldn't be able to make it, please do let me know.

萬一你不能來，拜託一定要告訴我。

⓯ A covered dish for 6-8 people will be appreciated.

請大家各自帶一道菜，大約六到八人份量。

⓰ Dress code: casual attire / all white / something red...
著裝規定：便裝／全身白／紅色的東西……

⓱ Proper attire is required at the restaurant.
餐廳需要穿著正式服裝。

⓲ Children / Pets are welcome.
歡迎小孩／寵物參加。

慣用語與句型應用指南

❶ BYOB　自己帶酒

"Bring your own beer/bottle/booze" 的縮寫。

▶ Feel free to **BYOB**.
可以自己帶要喝的酒。

❷ for the world　（強調）為了任何理由

口語化的"for any reason"

▶ I wouldn't miss your birthday party **for the world**.
我不可能為了任何理由錯過你的生日派對（我一定會去的）。

❸ How's life (treating you)?　（非正式）你過得好嗎？

▶ Haven't seen you for a while! **How's life treating you**?
好陣子不見了！過得好嗎？

❹ Please join us for a celebration of...　請一同來慶賀……

▶ **Please join us a celebration of** love and friendship.
請與我們一同歡慶愛與友情。

❺ You can't miss it.　不可能會沒看見、沒注意到某事、某物。

▶ It's a red building. **You can't miss it**.
那是一棟紅色建築，你一定會看到的。

單字片語應用指南

❶ attire （正式、特定的）服裝衣著

▶ Proper **attire** is required at the Michelin-starred restaurant.
在這間米其林餐廳用餐要著正式服裝。

▶ Not only club members but also visitors are required to wear formal golf **attire**.
包括俱樂部會員以及訪客都必須著正式高爾夫服裝。

❷ fancy （英式用法）表示喜歡

★美式用法：**like**

▶ I really **fancy** the last collection that Zara has released, so beautiful!
我真的很喜歡 Zara 推出的最新系列，超美的！

❸ flat （英式用法）公寓

★美式用法：**apartment**

▶ I am looking for a furnished **flat** in London.
我正在尋覓倫敦有附傢俱的公寓。

❹ in case 以防萬一

▶ Bring some money just **in case**.
帶點錢在身上吧，以防萬一。

❺ pudding （英式用法）非正式，口語意思有以下幾種：

一餐中最後一道甜點

▶ Can you bring trifle for **pudding**?
你能帶奶油鬆糕來當飯後甜點嗎？

（用肉加麵粉做成的）香腸類食物；布丁（非甜品）

▶ black pudding 黑布丁（血腸）

- ▶ Yorkshire pudding　約克夏布丁
- ▶ steak and kidney pudding　牛排腰子派

💬 娜娜老師的寫作小撇步

回覆接受邀請的簡短金句：

- ▶ I wouldn't miss it for the world.
  我絕對不可能錯過這個的。

- ▶ I am more than happy to attend your retirement party.
  Please let me know if I can bring something.
  我很開心，會出席您的退休派對。請讓我知道我需要帶點什麼東西過去。

- ▶ It's very thoughtful of you to organize the event and of
  course we will be there for you.
  你舉辦這個活動，真的好貼心，我們一定會出席的。

How Have You Been? Keep Your Long-distance Friendship Alive

你最近好嗎？維持你的遠距離友情

現代生活腳步繁忙，感覺好像才不過一轉眼的時間，其實一年已經過去了，若想跟世界各地朋友維繫感情，社群網路平台讓現代人得以突破時空的限制，本帖提供你許多溫馨、幽默的英文句子，讓你可以跟全世界各地的朋友盡情地說嗨。

 小提醒大領悟 Reminders

不在身邊時常往來的朋友，時間一久即使想要問候對方，都覺得有點怪，因為不知道能說什麼，其實只要透過幾個小方式，友誼的橋樑還是可以保持順暢。

❶ **問候對方的家人（如果你與對方的家人有共同回憶）**

▶ How's Ewan going? Is he still complaining about the weather all the time? Say hello to Ewan for me.

Ewan 過得如何呢？他是不是還在天天抱怨天氣啊？幫我跟他問好。

❷ **詢問共同朋友的消息**

▶ Have you heard from Lucy?

你有聽說 Lucy 的消息嗎？

▶ Are you still in touch with Cathy?

你有跟 Cathy 聯絡嗎？

❸ 談論最近流行的電影、電視劇或是你們彼此共同的興趣

▶ Have you seen *Avengers* 4?

《復仇者聯盟 4》你看過了沒？

❹ 多變化的結尾用詞

與熟人或朋友間的信件，結尾語同樣在傳達情誼與關心，像是 "Lots of Love（很多的愛）"、"Big Hugs（大大的擁抱）" 或是 "xoxo（親親擁抱之意）" 等等都可以。

 書信寫作步驟 Step by Step

STEP 1　打個招呼

How have you been? It's been ages since we met up last Christmas in London!

你最近好嗎？自從我們上次在倫敦過聖誕，已經多久沒見了呀！

STEP 2　分享自己生活並問候對方

I am now living in Hong Kong with my wife, Jessie. Have you been to Hong Kong before? How's your research going? I remember you telling me that you were planning to go to India. Have you finished your field research already?

我跟我老婆 Jessie 現在住在香港，你有來過香港嗎？你研究進行得如何了？我記得你跟我說過你打算去印度一趟，那邊的田野調查告一段落了嗎？

STEP 3　進一步提議

Want to FaceTime this weekend?

這週末要視訊一下嗎？

STEP 4 溫馨結尾

Hope to hear from you soon. Give my love to your family.
希望很快有你的消息，祝福你的家人。

情 境 Situation

這天晚上你在 Instagram 動態上看到當年留學認識的英國朋友 Amy 在酒吧慶生，你想起在異鄉與朋友相伴的日子，很想透過訊息來傳遞你的思念與祝福。

範 例 Example

Dear Amy,

How have you been? It's been ages since we had the perfect Christmas dinner in London. I miss you so bad. Hope everything goes well with you.

Guess what! I quit my job and started my own business. Finally, I know. YEAH! I finally decided to chase my dream. It's tough but exciting and rewarding. It feels so right when we finally do the thing we always want to do.

How about you? Are you still working at NHS? I can't wait to hear all about it.

Hey, why not we Skype sometime? Say next weekend? Let me know. It would be GREAT to catch up!

Lots of Love,
Serena

親愛的 Amy，

你近來好嗎？自從在倫敦那次完美的聖誕晚餐之後已經好久不見了，好想你喔，希望你一切都很好。

你知道嗎？我辭職了，開始創業，終於，哈哈！還記得我以前老是抱怨我的工作嗎？我只能說，我準備「擁抱新的人生」了！我終於決定要追求夢想。一切都很辛苦，但是很興奮、很值得。當我們終於做自己想做的事情，這種感覺真的是太棒了！

你呢？你還在 NHS 工作嗎？真想知道你的近況。

嘿，要不要 Skype 聊天呢？下週末如何？看怎樣你再跟我說好了，可以聊聊一定超棒！

很多的愛，
Serena

實用例句應用指南

❶ **How's it going**? I hope you're doing well/fine.
最近如何？希望你一切都好。

❷ **It's been a while** since we've seen each other. Hope everything is going well with you.
好久不見了，希望你一切都很順心呀！

❸ Hope you are well. I'm sorry I haven't been in touch for such a long time.

希望你都好。不好意思已經隔了好一陣子沒聯絡了。

❹ How are you? **I miss you so bad**.

你好不好啊？我超想你的。

❺ Hey butthead, I miss you already.

嘿，「大頭蛋」（暱稱），已經開始想你了。

❻ I miss spending time with you.

想念跟你膩在一起的日子。

❼ A funny thing happened to me... Are you still working at NHS[1]? Is everything going fine?

跟你講個好笑的事情……你還在 NHS 工作嗎？一切順利嗎？

❽ I've got some good news! I finally got admission from UCL. I am so excited but a bit nervous about moving to London. Flat hunting is like a nightmare.

我有好消息！我申請到 UCL（University of London）了，很興奮也有點緊張，要搬到倫敦去。找房子真是一場惡夢。

❾ I heard a rumor that you would be visiting Taiwan this summer.

聽說你好像這個夏天要來台灣玩。

❿ **We should meet up sometime**.

我們應該找時間碰個面。

---

[1] NHS；National Health Service 國民健保署

❶ It's been ages... 已經好久……

"ages" 在這邊表示一段很長的時間。在口語表達上，朋友如果隔了一陣子沒有相約，再度碰面很興奮的時候也可以這麼說。

▶ **It's been ages**!
超久沒見的啦！

❷ I miss you so bad 我非常想你；想死你了

"I miss you so much" 是很常見的，這邊換一個說法，用 "bad" 來表示，這邊的意思跟「壞」沒有關係，就是代表「非常；極度」的意思。

▶ Welcome back! **I miss you so bad**!
歡迎回來！我想死你了！

❸ I was going to... 本來要……（後來沒有發生）

▶ **I was going to** tell you that the shop was closed yesterday.
我本來要跟你說（實際上沒說），那家店昨天沒開。

❶ be/get/keep/stay in touch (with someone)
跟某人保持聯繫、溝通（透過電話、電子郵件等）

▶ We have to **keep in touch** with our potential clients.
我們必須跟潛在客戶保持聯繫。

❷ meet up 碰面

▶ I suggest that we **meet up** at McDonald's.
我提議我們在麥當勞碰面。

❸ catch up 聚聚；聊聊

▶ It's really nice meeting you at Serena's Party last night. We should **catch up** sometimes.
昨晚在 Serena 的派對上認識你真是太好了，我們應該找時間聚聚。

Ask Friends for Advice
向朋友詢問建議

當我們在工作或生活上遇到問題，自然會想到朋友圈裡可能有誰能夠提供協助，詢問的事情天南地北，很難包山包海詳列出來，大家可以針對自己的情況來斟酌修改例句。

 小提醒大領悟 Reminders

#MakeItClear

哪怕你覺得請教的問題對於對方來說可能很容易回答，除非是非常親密的朋友，否則這類訊息都應該說明清楚，而不是隨便幾個字就發出去，不然對方也難免會有被當成 Google 的感覺了。

#KeepThemInTheLoop

記得，讓對方知道後續進展是有禮貌的表現，別讓對方覺得回覆了你後就像把石頭扔到海裡一樣無消無息，有被利用、過河拆橋的感覺。

 書信寫作步驟 Step by Step

STEP 1　開場白

❶ **不是很熟可以用共同友人當作橋樑，例如：**

How have you been? It was so nice to see you and Amy at

the Christmas party last month.

你好嗎？上個月耶誕派對好開心見到你跟 Amy。

❷ **有交情可以透過問候對方的狀況或是討論共通話題，例如：**

How's going? Have you finished those Taekwon-Do classes? Guess what? I just signed up for that last week. Can you believe it? I mean, I can't even remember when was the last time I went to the gym.

最近如何？你的跆拳道課程上完了嗎？我上禮拜竟然也報名耶，你相信嗎？我連我上次去健身房是什麼時候都不記得了。

STEP 2　簡短聊聊自己（為了下一個步驟做準備）

After putting up with the noise for three months, I have decided to live off-campus. I've been looking for a room in a shared flat since May, but flat hunting is like a nightmare.

這三個月我實在受夠這些噪音了，我想要搬到校外的分租宿舍，從五月開始找房子找到現在，但是找房子真的是一場惡夢。

STEP 3　直接提問

Amy told me the other day that you are looking for a flatmate. I was wondering if you've found prospective flatmates or not. If not, I was thinking that perhaps we could share the flat together. What do you think?

Amy 那天跟我說你正在找房子，不知道你找到室友了嗎？如果沒有，我們或許可以一起租房子，你覺得如何呢？

STEP 4　道謝 （給對方不同提供你幫助的選項）

If you happen to know someone who is letting rooms, any information would be appreciated.

如果你剛好知道有誰在分租房間，不管你可以分享給我什麼消息，我都非常感謝。

你剛到國外讀書幾個月，常常熬夜寫報告論文，學校宿舍隔音很差，需要專心的你被吵到快要往生，開始想要找外面的房子，英國朋友 Amy 剛好告訴你，他朋友 Jon 好像在找室友，你覺得可以問問看，但是你跟 Jon 其實不熟⋯⋯

範 例 Example

Hi Jon,

How have you been? It was so nice to see you and Amy at the Christmas party last month.

After putting up with the noise for three months, I have decided to live off-campus. I've been looking for a room in a shared flat since May. Flat hunting is just like a nightmare. Amy told me the other day that you are looking for a flatmate. I was wondering if you've found prospective flatmates or not. If not, I was thinking that perhaps we could share the flat together. What do you think?

Or, **if you happen to know** someone who is letting rooms or looking for a flatmate, any information would be appreciated.

Thanks,
Serena

哈囉 Jon，

最近如何？上個月很開心跟你和 Amy 在耶誕派對上見面。

這三個月我實在忍受夠宿舍的噪音了，我想要搬到校外的分租宿舍。可是我從五月開始找了一陣子了，沒有找到合適的。找房子就跟惡夢一樣，Amy 跟我講你好像在找室友，我在想不知你找到室友了嗎？如果沒有，我們或許可以一起租房子。你覺得如何呢？

還是如果你剛好知道有誰在分租房間或是找室友，不管你可以分享給我什麼消息，我都非常感謝。

謝謝，
Serena

實用例句應用指南

❶ I hope **all is well**. Thank you for those "surviving tips" you taught me. It helps a lot.
希望一切安好。謝謝你之前教我的「生存撇步」，超級有用的。

❷ **If you don't mind, would you**...?
如果你不介意的話，你可以⋯⋯嗎？

❸ **I was wondering if you could put me in touch with** your friend, James, who also works in Japan?
你方便介紹我認識你那位也在日本工作的朋友 James 嗎？

❹ As you probably can tell, I am still booking for a position as a marketing representative.
你應該知道，我還在找銷售代表的工作。

❺ I would appreciate it if you can think of any contacts you might be able to put me in touch with.
如果你可以想到可能可以介紹給我的相關人士，我會非常感激你的。

❻ If you don't feel comfortable passing along Katie's contact information, it's okay and I totally understand.

要是你覺得介紹 Katie 給我認識有些不妥的話，沒關係我可以理解。

❼ I know that you must be very busy at the end of the semester, if not, I totally understand.

知道你現在是學期末一定很忙，如果你不能幫忙我，我完全可以理解。

慣用語與句型應用指南

❶ **All is well.** **一切安好。**

▶ I hope **all is well** with you.
我希望你一切安好。

▶ "The scar had not pained Harry for nineteen years. **All was well**."

— J.K. Rowling, *Harry Potter and the Deathly Hallows*"
十九年了，這塊疤痕再也沒有痛過。一切安好。

—J.K. 羅琳《哈利波特：死神的聖物》

❷ **I hope you're doing great/well.**
用來問候對方，「希望你一切都好」的說法。

▶ The upcoming exams must drive you crazy! I **hope you're doing well**.
即將到來的考試一定讓你快瘋了！我希望你一切都好。

❸ **I was wondering if/weather** **表達客氣、委婉之意**

用 "was" 不是表示過去時間發生的事情，而是禮貌口吻，小心不要寫成 "I am wondering"。

▶ **I was wondering if/whether** you'd like to have dinner with me tomorrow night?
明天晚上不知道你願不願意與我共進晚餐呢？

❹ Keep... in the loop. 希望得知事件的後續進展與消息

"loop" 當名詞是迴圈、圓圈、環形的意思。當我們對別人說 "Keep me in the loop"，意指請把我納入那個小圈裡面，像是 "Keep me updated." 或 "Keep me posted."。

▶ Best wishes for your new life in Edinburgh! **Keep** me **in the loop**.
祝你在愛丁堡的新生活一切都好！要向我報告喔。

單字片語應用指南

❶ in touch (with someone) 與某人聯繫（見面、通話、書信等）

▶ Are you still **in touch with** friends from college?
你還有跟大學的朋友聯絡嗎？

put somebody in touch with someone
為某人「牽線」認識別人

▶ My friend Amy **put me in touch with** a real estate agent.
我朋友 Amy 幫我介紹一位地產經紀人。

keep/stay in touch 保持聯絡（即使彼此不一定能常常見面）

▶ Let's **keep in touch** after graduation!
我們畢業之後繼續保持聯絡吧！

get in touch 在沒有見面之後「開始」連絡

▶ I tried to **get in touch** with Doctor Lee, but he hasn't replied my email.
我嘗試著聯繫李博士，但是都還沒有回音。

❷ sign up for 報名參加某（有組織規劃的）活動。

▶ I have **signed up for** dancing classes at the community college.
我已經報名社區大學的舞蹈課。

Ask for Something Back Politely
想要回東西的禮貌說法

熟人之間的訊息往來通常隨性，不過，有時候我們要詢問的事情或許會比較難以啟齒，像是請對方還錢，或是請對方歸還借出的物品，而且你還不確定他到底還給你了沒……

 小提醒大領悟 Reminders

#KeepCalm #BeStraightForward

其實真的不用覺得「尷尬」，把事情整理清楚並不是什麼壞事，也不用一廂情願要做爛好人，如果是錢這種相對比較敏感的事情，面對面溝通通常比較好，可以降低造成誤會的機率。

 書信寫作步驟 Step by Step

STEP 1　提醒事發始末

▶ I'm looking for my copy of *Harry Potter*, do you still have it?
我在找我的《哈利波特》那本書，有在你那邊嗎？

STEP 2　簡單告訴對方你的情況

▶ I'm rereading the series because I want to post reviews on my blog.
我現在重讀整個系列，因為我想在部落格上發心得文。

你記得你之前借給同學 Helen 一本小說，但是已經過了太久你根本也想不起來他到底還你了沒。那本書你最近寫報告的時候需要用，到處翻箱倒櫃都找不到，是該提起勇氣問一下 Helen 了……

 範 例 Example

Hi Helen,

How are you? I am working on my essay at the moment and I need the copy of *Gone Girl*. I couldn't find it. Do you still have the copy of *Gone Girl* that I lent you? Are you still using it? If not, I was thinking I could have it back this weekend.

xx,
Serena

嗨 Helen，

哈囉！我正在努力寫報告，我很需要《控制》那本小說，卻到處都找不到。是不是還在你那邊呀？你還在看嗎？如果沒有，我想要這個週末跟你拿回來。

親親，
Serena

❶ Do you still have [item] that I lent you? Are you still using it?

我的 [東西、物件] 有在你那邊嗎？你還有要用嗎？

❷ I'd like to have my copy of *Twilight* back next week if that's okay with you.

如果方便的話，《暮光之城》那本書我想拿回來。

❸ Do you remember that I loaned [item] to you last month? Would you mind giving xxx back to me?

還記得上個月我借你的 [東西、物件] 嗎？方便還給我嗎？

❹ Have you finished reading the book by Ang Li I lent you?

我借你那本李安的書你看完了嗎？

❺ Actually, I was hoping that I could have it back if you don't need it anymore because I wanted to use it for [purpose].

如果你不需要的話，其實我想拿回來，因為我要用來 [做……（用途）]。

❻ I have fallen behind with my rent, and I'm really depending on you paying me back to make that payment.

我已經遲繳房租了，我需要你還我錢，不然我繳不出來。

❼ Are you done with [item]? Could I borrow it back? Pretty please?

你用完 [東西、物件] 了嗎？我可以跟你「借」回來嗎？拜託拜託？（幽默語氣）

慣用語與句型應用指南

❶ get it back / bring it back to　將東西、物件帶來、歸還。

注意不要跟 "get back to" 搞混，get back to 是短時間之內回覆對方的意思（通常是電話），像是：

▶ Can you **get** my book **back to** me by next Monday?
你下星期一可以帶我的書還我嗎？

▶ I will **get back to** you later after I finish this email.
等我寫完這封信我去找（回電）給你。

❷ **Would you mind Ving** （禮貌用法）你介意去做……嗎？

記得 "mind" 後面是加動名詞 Ving，不要寫錯了。

▶ **Would you mind opening** the window?
你介意開窗戶嗎？

你也可以寫成：

▶ **Would you mind** if I **opened** the window?
你介意我打開窗戶嗎？

這邊 "opened" 用過去式動詞也是表示禮貌，書寫上建議這麼寫。不過，口語上是會聽到後面接現在式，像是：

▶ **Would you mind** if I **sit** here?
你介意我坐在這邊嗎？

單字片語應用指南

❶ **copy** （書報、印刷品）一本；一冊

▶ Our professor has requested us to buy a **copy** of her book before the next lecture.
我們的教授要求我們下次上課前要買一本她的書。

❷ **done** （形容詞）完成的；做完的

▶ The job is almost **done**.
工作幾乎要完成囉。

▶ Is the job done yet?
工作做了嗎？

▶ Are you **done** with my copy of *Twilight*?
我的《暮光之城》你看完了嗎？

❸ loan 借出

▶ Thank you so much for the **loan** of your car.
謝謝你把車子借給我。

▶ I **loaned** my sister 5,000 pounds last month.
上個月我借給我妹妹五千英鎊。

❹ Pretty please? （口語的幽默表示）拜託拜託？

當你想說服或是請求對方，並且要讓自己表現出友善、幽默的樣子。

▶ Can I take a sip of your milkshake? **Pretty please**?
我可以喝一口你的奶昔嗎？拜託拜託？

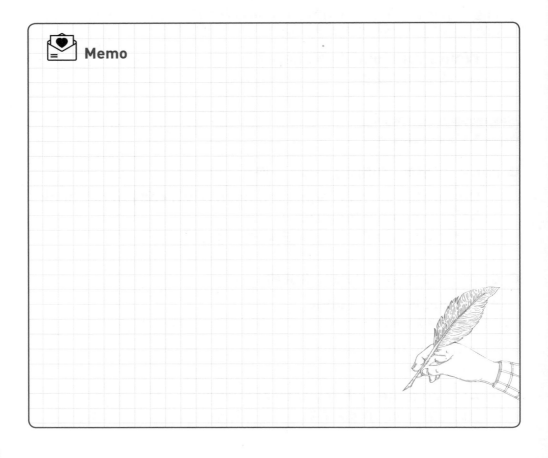

Memo

PLEASE 請

❶ disappear/vanish into thin air
（查無原因）消失得無影無蹤

❷ someone's hands are tied 受到限制

❸ burst into something 突然開始

❹ make someone's acquaintance 初次相識

❺ turn to someone 請求幫忙

❻ hear from someone 從某人得知消息

❼ catch/strike someone's fancy
贏得對方的喜歡、興趣

❽ Please note that.. 請注意……

❾ make matters worse 讓事情變得更糟

❿ mess up 搞砸；弄懂

⓫ take the time 花費力氣去（做某件事）

⓬ keep...in the loop 希望得知事件的後續進展與消息

Part 2

THANK YOU 謝謝

好禮貌運動
關於「感謝」與「祝福」溫馨大集合

商務篇 BUSINESS

 # 熟人篇 FRIENDS

Thank You Note

通用感謝函

在職場上，"thank you"兩個字彷彿是基本禮貌而已，當然不足以清楚表達你想傳達的感謝，來看看本帖幫你整理的實用感謝例句。

 小建議大思考 Suggestions

❶ 手寫會讓信件更有溫度。

❷ 感謝信如果言過其實、油腔滑調，反而像是在阿諛奉承，會有反效果。

#Happiness #Warmth #AmitKumar

德州大學奧斯丁分校（University of Texas at Austin）的教授Amit Kumar，針對"Happiness（幸福感）"做了研究，發現人們普遍低估一封感謝信函會帶給對方多好的感受，也過於擔心是否措辭適當與否，訪談結果發現大部分的收件者並不是太在意措辭，而是因為那份"Warmth（暖心的情意）"。

書信寫作步驟 Step by Step

STEP 1　道謝

We would like to take this opportunity to thank you for
giving us the chance to work with you.
謝謝您給予我們合作的機會。

STEP 2　說明對方的貢獻

Due to your continued support, we are able to meet our
obligations to our suppliers and provide superior service to
our customers.
因為您持續的支持,我們得以實踐對供應商的承諾,並且提供客戶最優質的服務。

STEP 3　預祝未來或其他聯繫事宜

Thank you again for your hard work and commitment to our
company. With your support, we are certain that we will be
equally successful.
再次謝謝您對本公司的努力付出與支持。有您的支持,我們確信我們能共同締造佳績。

 情 境 Situation

你負責專案的客戶與你長期合作,關係一直非常良好,最近剛好是又一次的合作企劃成功告一段落,你覺得可以趁這個機會寫一封溫馨的感謝信,但你不希望這封感謝信就像千篇一律的賀卡一樣流於形式……

Hi Mr. Lee,

We would like to take this opportunity to thank you for giving us the chance to work with you. Together we celebrated our eighth anniversary and we would like to let you know that because of your support, it has been an amazing adventure. Due to your continued commitment, we are able to meet our obligations to our suppliers and provide superior service to our customers.

Thank you once again.

We look forward to working with you in the years to come, and wish your company continued success.

Warm Regards,
Serena

親愛的 Lee 先生，

我們想藉此機會感謝您與我們合作。歡慶我們的合作邁入第八年頭，因為您的支持，一路以來如此精彩。因為您的支持，我們得以實踐對供應商的承諾，並且提供客戶最優質的服務。

再次感謝您。

我們期待與您共創美好未來，也祝福貴公司業績蒸蒸日上一路長紅。

溫暖的問候，
Serena

實用例句應用指南

❶ Through collaboration, we together have achieved better results.
因為業務合作，我們一起達成更好的業績。

❷ We wouldn't be here without loyal customers like you.
我們能有今天，都要歸功於有您這樣的忠實顧客。

❸ Your generous donation **made a big difference**.
您慷慨的捐助帶來莫大影響。

❹ **We are deeply indebted to you** for your donation.
我們誠摯的感謝您的捐獻。

❺ **I would like to express my gratitude for** your generous hospitality on my last trip to London.
我想對於我上次出差去倫敦時，您的盛情款待表示感激。

❻ **On behalf of [name/title],** I'd like to thank you for your great cooperation.
謹代表 [名字／頭銜]，對於您的鼎力協助我們表示感謝。

❼ **Thank you for your continued support. We wish your company continued success and prosperity**.
謝謝您的支持照顧，祝福您公司蓬勃發展、順利成功。

❽ **Thank you for sharing your valuable experience with our members.**
感謝您分享您的寶貴經驗予我們的成員。

❾ (I'm writing this letter to kindly) Thank you for inviting me to attend the ABC event/conference in Taipei.
（我寫這封信是想）謝謝您邀請我參加台北的 ABC 活動／研討會。

❿ Thank you for your active participation and valuable insights. We hope that you found the event/meeting/conference/workshop informative and worthwhile.

謝謝您的積極參與與見解，希望這個活動／會議／研討會／工作坊對您來說是訊息豐富、不虛此行。

⓫ We are so grateful that you helped us **get a foot in the door**.

感激您幫助我們成功踏入這個產業。

慣用語與句型應用指南

❶ get a/your foot in the door 通過門檻

想像一名業務員挨家挨戶推銷產品，會一腳踩進去，不讓對方很快把家門關上，這個意思就是用來描述人們為了達到目標而跨出成功的第一步。

▶ Fresh graduates need to **get a foot in the door**.
社會新鮮人需要一個入門的機會。

❷ make a (big) difference / make a world of difference
帶來大幅改變；帶來重大意義

▶ Doing exercise regularly can **make a big difference** to your state of health.
規律運動會大大改善你的健康狀況。

▶ Your support **made a world of difference**.
您的支持帶來莫大助益。

not make any difference / make no difference
沒有差別；不會帶來影響

▶ Go ahead. Ask him again if you want, but it won't make any difference.
去啊，再去問他一次，但是結果不會變的。

❸ We're indebted to you for 我們很感激您……

▶ **We are** all entirely **indebted to you for** your donation.
我們都非常感激您的捐助。

❶ fresh graduate 大學畢業生

▶ She will be a **fresh graduate** next June.
她在明年六月即將是個大學畢業生。

❷ an entry-level job candidate 職場新鮮人

▶ As **an entry-level job candidate**, Joan has beaten other experienced staff to the final interview.
作為一個職場新鮮人，Joan 已經打敗了其他經驗豐富的員工，來到最後的面試。

❸ patronage 贊助；資助

▶ We are grateful for your continued **patronage**.
感謝您的持續贊助。

❹ [time] to come 即將到來的

▶ in the **days/weeks/years to come**
在接下來的幾天／幾週／幾年

Thank You Message for Colleagues/Employees

給同事／員工的感謝訊息

接受「同事」的幫忙之後，除了口頭一聲謝謝之外，發一封溫馨感謝的郵件，是基本的禮貌，也能夠促進此後互助合作的正向默契。

如果你身為「主管」，掌握時機感謝團隊成員，是認可下屬在工作上的價值與貢獻，也同時看重對方付出的時間與心力。

 小建議大思考 Suggestions

#好事傳天下

如果是要感謝特定同事協助，寄出這封信的同時，可以考慮副本給對方的主管，如果是要感謝特定一位員工，在公司聚餐晚宴上公開感謝也是一個方式。

#AThankyouNoteGoesALongWay #AdrianGostick #ChesterElton

暢銷書作家 Adrian Gostick 和 Chester Elton 一系列的「胡蘿蔔管理法」強調的就是「獎勵」的藝術，讓員工了解他們的工作價值比起光是發薪水或獎金來得更重要。有效激勵員工不僅可以「降低人員流動率（lower employee turnover）」、「提高顧客滿意度（higher customer satisfaction）」，還能同時「提高員工的參與程度（higher worker engagement levels）」。

書信寫作步驟 Step by Step

STEP 1　謝謝對方幫忙

I really appreciate the effort and extra time you put into our project.

我很感激您為了我們的專案付出的額外時間與努力。

STEP 2　描述事實肯定對方貢獻

Without your hard work, talents, and skills, we wouldn't have been able to achieve this together.

沒有您的努力，天分以及技能，我們將不可能完成任務。

STEP 3　補充

I will send you a follow-up when this project is completed. Please let me know if and when I can return the favor.

當這個專案完成之後，我會寄給您後續發展情形。請讓我知道我能如何，及何時可以回報您。

 情 境 A Situation A

提案截止日在即，你的電腦系統竟然扯你後腿，菜鳥不能犯的錯誤就是沒有備份，你懊悔不已，只能求助資訊部門的同事盡快幫你把檔案復原，另外想著怎麼補救，沒想到隔天一早，你驚喜的發現一切回到原樣，你埋頭發揮最高效率，在最後一刻即時把工作完成，後來才知道，原來那位同事為了你的電腦加班了好幾個小時，你知道之後親自去道謝，又覺得，應該要寫一封信好好感謝對方的支持與協助……

Hello Michael,

You literally saved my life. Thank you so much for the tremendous support. Thanks to you, we handed in our proposal just in time and we are expecting the result.

And I just learned that you even worked late to repair the system. **I can't thank you enough.** I deeply appreciate all the extra time and effort you put in and I am fortunate to have you as a colleague.

Thank you again and please let me know if and when I can return the favor.

All the best,
Serena

哈囉麥可，

你簡直救了我的命。超級感謝你幫我修電腦，沒有你，我根本不可能做到。因為你，我們才能準時交稿，我們正在等提案結果。

我剛剛才知道你為了這件事情還加班維修系統，我謝你謝不完的。我非常感激你付出額外時間與投注精力協助我，有你這樣的同事，我真的很幸運。

再次感謝你，也請讓我知道何時以及如何我有可能回報你。

祝福你，
Serena

情 境 **B** Situation B

身為新創團隊亞太區主管的你,感恩節將至,你想藉由這個機會表達你對團隊成員的感謝。

 範 例 Example

Deaar Colleagues,

My heartfelt thanks to all of you for your energy, innovation and commitment to our vision. Your contribution and hard work have not gone unnoticed and I would like to express my sincere gratitude to every one of you.

Without a great team, all leaders are nothing. I have been fortunate to work with such a stellar team. Please know how proud I am to serve you as the leader of Marketing. COM, and I am greatly thankful to face challenges and achieve goals alongside you.

Thank you for your continued dedication.

My sincere best wishes to you and your family for the holidays.
Serena

親愛的同事們,

誠心感謝各位的投入、創新以及對我們願景的承諾。你們的貢獻與努力工作不會被忽視,我誠摯地向你們每一個人致謝。

沒有團隊，就沒有領導者。我相當幸運能與如此精彩的團隊共事。我感到非常驕傲能帶領 Marketing. COM，而我更感激能與你們一同面對挑戰達成目標。

謝謝你們一直以來持續的付出。

祝福您與您的家人佳節愉快，

Serena

實用例句應用指南

❶ I would like to express my personal gratitude for the energy and extra time you put into our project.
我想向您表達我個人的感激，謝謝您為了我們的專案所付出的時間跟精神。

❷ Thank you for your tremendous help.
謝謝您幫了我們一個大忙。

❸ Thank you for **showing me the ropes**.
謝謝你幫我進入狀況。

❹ I appreciate the time you've taken from your own work and I am fortunate to have you as a colleague.
我感激你撥冗來幫助我，有你這樣的同事，我感到幸運。

❺ Your excellent problem-solving skills help us thrive on stressful and looming deadlines.
您絕佳的問題解決能力幫助我們在截止日期壓力逼近的當下，能發揮到最好。

❻ Without your support, we wouldn't have removed the roadblocks.
沒有你的支持，我們無法克服這些阻礙。

❼ This campaign had remained at a standstill before you joined us and thank you for being patient with us during this **nerve-racking** process.

在您加入之前，這個案子幾乎就在一個僵局裡面，在這個令人煩心的過程中，謝謝您的耐心。

❽ To be honest, the situation is deadlocked and your suggestions are very helpful for us to **increase the speed of** decision making.

坦白說，我們面臨一個僵局，而你的建議非常有助益，我們因此可以加快決策的腳步。

❾ **Thanks for stepping in**. We do need a different approach toward collaboration.

謝謝你加入，這是一個完美的時機，我們正需要一個不同的方式來達成合作。

慣用語與句型應用指南

❶ go a long way / go far　未來會很順利；前程遠大

▶ Colin is a very talented musician. We all believe that he will **go far**.

Colin 是一位很有才華的音樂家，我們相信他未來會大有成就。

---

❷ has/have gone unnoticed...　未被察覺

▶ Tim is so good at spotting problems that otherwise would **have gone unnoticed**.

Tim 很擅長發覺那些難以察覺的問題。

---

❸ show someone the ropes　指導某人如何做（事情）

rope 這裡不是繩子的意思，而是表示規則、準則或技巧程序。

know the ropes　對某事務工作很了解、很有經驗。

▶ Go ask Mr. Chang. He **knows the ropes**.

去問張先生，他很有經驗的。

learn the ropes　還在學習、了解做事情的方法

▶ Be patient! **Learning the ropes** takes some time.
有點耐心！要學習事情基本面總要花點時間。

❶ deadlocked　（雙方不願退讓；沒有共識）僵持不下的

▶ The situation has been **deadlocked** for several months.
情況僵持不下數月。

❷ nerve-racking　讓人煩心的

▶ Application process is a **nerve-racking** experience.
申請過程是令人煩心的經驗。

❸ roadblock　路障；（在事情進行上的）障礙

▶ Removing those **roadblocks** will make it easier for team members to do their jobs.
清除阻礙會讓團隊成員更容易完成任務。

❹ standstill　停滯不前的

▶ I think my career is at a **standstill**.
我覺得我的職涯發展呈現停滯狀態。

❺ thrive　成長繁盛

▶ Our business has successfully **thrived** because of recent marketing campaigns.
因為最近的行銷活動，我們的生意已經開始茁壯成長。

▶ Some people seem to **thrive** on stress.
有些人似乎在壓力底下表現很好。

Thank Someone for a Referral or Recommendation

感謝某人引薦（工作機會）或推薦（客戶）

在職場人脈關係當中，如果能被引薦是非常值得感謝的。對方花了時間幫你聯繫關鍵人士，把自己的人脈資訊分享給你，你除了記得來日有機會要回饋對方之外，此刻應當誠心表達感謝。

 小建議大思考 Suggestions

表達感謝引薦的目的不只是道謝，應當視情況讓對方知道他對你帶來實際上的影響，假設是引薦工作，那面試進展如何呢？如果是引薦潛在客戶，見面後晤談情況如何呢？這些問題可以讓你的信更令人印象深刻。

 書信寫作步驟 Step by Step

STEP 1　說明感謝幫忙

Thank you for taking the time to share your experience with me and introducing me to Tim Smith, product marketing manager at Ideal Strategy.

謝謝您花時間與我分享您的精彩經歷，還幫我引薦給理想策略公司的產品行銷經理 Tim Smith。

STEP 2　補充近況

I would like to share good news with you. I will meet with the hiring manager later this week for a second interview.

想跟您分享一個好消息,我這個禮拜會跟招聘經理第二次面試。

STEP 3　再次感謝

Thank you very much for your kindness and help. I will keep you posted on how the interview goes and do my best to live up to your expectations.

再次感謝您的幫助。我會讓您知道面試的後續發展,也一定不會辜負您的期望。

 情 境 **A** Situation A

你一直對行銷工作很有興趣,想起一位長輩在行銷領域有相當資歷,你不久前鼓起勇氣向對方請教,沒想到對方不僅請你喝了咖啡,還將你的名字跟經歷引薦給他認識的某位行銷經理,你感到受寵若驚,想要好好寫一封信,真誠的告訴對方,你相當感激他所為你做的,你也希望可以跟他保持聯繫,日後希望能有機會回報。

 範 例 Example

Dear Mr. Gordon,

Thank you for the fantastic conversation. I appreciate your willingness to meet with me. I appreciate the time you spent discussing the job with me. Because of you, I learned a lot about this field and how to prepare for the hiring process. Based on your advice, I plan to update my resume to emphasize marketing-related experience and skills.

Also, I appreciate your kindness and support to introduce me to Tim Smith, product marketing manager at Ideal Strategy. I will keep you posted on how the interview goes.

I can't thank you enough and your support means a lot to me. I will send a LinkedIn invitation to make it easier for us to keep in touch. Again, thank you for your referral and I hope I can return the favor in the near future.

Sincerely,
Serena

親愛的 Gordon 先生，

與您晤談真是獲益良多，我很感激您願意與我碰面，也很感激您花時間與我討論這份工作，因為您，我更了解這個行業和要如何準備應徵相關職務。參照您的建議，我會更新我的履歷表，並且強調行銷相關的經驗與技能。

同時，我也很感激您把我介紹給理想策略公司的經理 Tim Smith，我也會讓您知道我申請工作的後續發展。

再多的感謝都不夠回報您的支持。我將會寄 LinkedIn 邀請給您，方便日後彼此聯繫。再次感謝您，也希望不遠的將來我能有機會能回報您。

誠摯地，
Serena

 情 境 B Situation B

你在一家新創小公司工作，專辦公司餐會茶點外匯，最需要的就是口碑推薦，其中一位客戶 Smith 小姐不僅連續兩個月的公司業務會議都選擇你的服務，還將你的公司推薦給她的往來客戶，這樣的舉動讓你倍受肯定，你要透過信件表達你的感激。

 範 例 Example

Dear Miss Smith,

Thank you very much for your referral. You have helped our business immensely. We appreciate your confidence in our catering service and it means a lot to us.

We won't let you down!

Thank you once again.

Sincerely,
Serena

親愛的 Smith 小姐，

非常感謝您的引薦，您帶給我們的業務莫大幫助，我們感謝您對我們外燴服務的肯定，這對我們來說意義深重。

我們將不會讓您們失望！

再次感謝您。

誠摯地，
Serena

實用例句應用指南

感謝對方引薦客戶給你

❶ Thank you for referring Delta Consultant to us for web design service.
謝謝您為我們的網頁設計引薦 Delta 顧問公司。

❷ I can't thank you enough for referring your friend Jane Smith to my firm.
真的非常感謝你介紹你的朋友 Jane Smith 來我的事務所。

❸ I really appreciate your **confidence in** our services.
我很感激您對我們業務的肯定。

感謝對方對你應徵工作上的幫忙

❹ Thank you for your valuable advice on how to achieve my career goal.
我很感激您提供我寶貴建議，幫助我達成我的職涯目標。

❺ I think my interview with the hiring manager went quite well and I look forward to the next steps in the hiring process.
我想我跟招聘經理的面談相當順利，我很期待應徵流程的後續發展。

感謝對方替你引薦關鍵人士

❻ **I appreciate your willingness to** introduce me to your contacts at Ideal Strategy.
我很感激您願意介紹引薦理想策略公司的相關人士讓我認識。

❼ I truly appreciate everything you've done for me.
我真的很感激您為我做的每件事。

❶ have confidence in someone　對某人有十足信心

▶ I **have confidence in** his ability to succeed.
我對他的成功有十足的信心。

❷ I appreciate your willingness to do somethings
我很感激您有這個意願去做某事……

▶ **I appreciate your willingness to** help out.
我感激您願意幫忙。

▶ **I appreciate your willingness to** meet with me.
我感激您願意與我會面。

❸ I can't thank you enough.
我怎麼謝謝你都不夠；我非常感謝你。

這種用否定句的方式寫的用法就跟 "I can't agree with you more.（我不能同意你更多；我非常同意你）" 一樣。

▶ **I can't thank you enough** for everything you have done for me.
我非常感謝您為我做的所有事情。

❹ keep in touch　保持聯絡

▶ My ex-wife and I still **keep in touch**.
我前妻跟我還是保持聯絡。

▶ Have you **kept in touch** with your college friends?
你還有跟大學朋友保持聯繫嗎？

❺ keep someone posted　（持續跟某人）更新最新近況

▶ I asked them to **keep me posted** on how this campaign is coming along.
我請他們持續向我更新這個活動的最新進展。

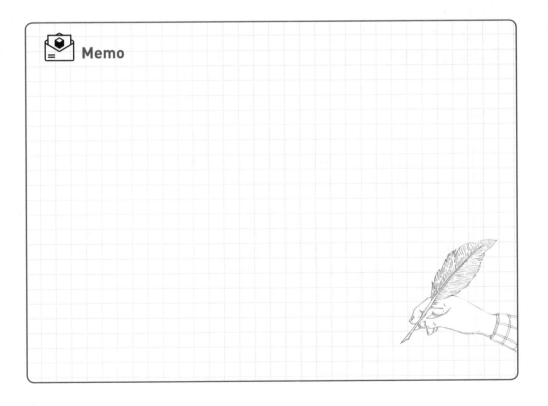

單字片語應用指南

❶ advice 建議

▶ 「提供」建議：offer (someone), give (someone), pass on, provide (someone with)

▶ 「接受」建議：take, get, receive

▶ 「尋求」建議：ask for, go to someone for, seek, turn to someone for

❷ live up to 履行（承諾）；（說到做到）實踐

▶ Her husband had no intention of **living up** to his promise.
她的丈夫一點也不想履行他的承諾。

✉ **Memo**

Thank You-Farewell

謝謝，珍重再見

即使職場環境中各式各樣的人來來去去，我們總有機會與幾個老面孔一起打拼，度過許多喜怒哀樂的日子。當那張老面孔要從崗位上退下，擁抱退休的第二人生，或是你自己有了新的機會要離職，邁向人生下一個階段，「再見」兩個字也是維繫人脈關係的重要一環，未來日子還很長，人際網絡是一輩子的，請看本帖分享如何寫一封道謝與祝福的道別信。

💬 小建議大思考 Suggestions

❶ 一定要走心

如果要退休的人是你很熟識的同僚長官，別忘了讚美對方並且感謝對方的幫助；假設是你要離職，這封道別信需要提及長官以及同僚對你的提攜，適切傳達感謝之情。

❷ 別忘了留下聯繫資訊

即將離職的你或是要退休的同事，都不會從專業市場及人際網路中消失不見，後會總是有期。

❸ 交代後續

如果你要離職，除了感謝之外，視業務情況需要提及接續你職位的人員及後續安排，讓收信方獲得充足資訊。

#歡送同事／長官退休

STEP 1 恭喜道賀

Congratulations on your retirement/achievement!
恭賀退休！

STEP 2 讚美對方，提及你自己與對方的共事回憶（若無可省略）

You are a true team leader. Regardless of our circumstances, you communicate openly with us, creating an environment of trust. **You make us feel valued.**
你是真正的領袖人才。無論面對什麼情況，你總能開明的與我們溝通，營造互信的團隊氣氛，你讓我們覺得備受重視。

STEP 3 溫馨祝福對方退休後的人生新篇章

I wish you **tons of happiness**. May your new chapter in life be more spectacular than you ever imagined.
希望你此後歡樂滿滿。祝你人生新篇章比你想像中的還要精彩萬分。

 情 境 A Situation A

公司的外籍顧問 Daniel 就要退休，歡送派對安排在月底舉行，你對於這個消息感到非常驚訝，你剛進這間公司時，曾經在這名外籍顧問領導下完成許多專案，一晃眼六年過去了，你總是感受到他熱情有幹勁的感染力，也很佩服他展現的縝密思維，你從他身上學到許多工作經驗與專業技巧，這封恭喜退休的信該怎麼寫呢？

Dear Daniel,

Congratulations on your retirement!

You are a true team leader. Regardless of our circumstances, you communicate openly with us, creating an environment of trust. You make us feel valued.

It has been such a pleasure working with you over the past 6 years. You've been an amazing mentor and a trustworthy friend, and we're sad to see you leave.

We wish you tons of happiness and may your new chapter in life be even more spectacular than you ever imagined.

Sincerely,
Serena

親愛的 Daniel，

退休恭喜！

您是真正的領袖人才。無論面對什麼情況，總能開明的與我們溝通，營造互信的團隊氣氛，您讓我們覺得備受重視。

過去六年來能有機會與您共事是我的榮幸，您是一位好棒的導師，也同時是一個很好的朋友，我們很捨不得跟您說再見。

祝福您此後歡樂滿滿，希望往後所有一切都精彩到超乎你的想像。

誠摯地，
Serena

#離職跟同事長官道別

STEP 1 告知離職事實

I am writing to let you know that **I will be leaving** ABC at the end of January / on January 31st .

我寫信是要跟你說一聲，我一月底／1 月 31 日要離開 ABC 公司。

STEP 2 道謝

（畫龍點睛，更多讚美文字請參考本帖的「實用例句應用指南」）

I'd like to express my sincere appreciation for your guidance and inspiration over the past five years. It's a pleasure to work with someone who knows how to build a high trust workplace. I am so grateful for the opportunity to work alongside you.

對於過去五年，我想藉此機會向您表達感謝，謝謝您給我的指教以及啟發。您懂得與他人建立信任並且營造激勵人心的工作環境，很榮幸與您共事，感謝有這個機會與您一起肩並肩作戰。

STEP 3 留下資訊以及再次道謝

You can always contact me at [email address] or [phone number]. Thank you again and I wish you all the best.

你可以透過 [電子信箱地址] 或 [手機號碼] 聯繫到我。再次感謝你，我祝福你一切順利。

 情 境 B Situation B

你才剛參加完外籍顧問 Daniel 的榮退派對，就接到獵人頭公司的好消息，決定要離職的你感到有點不捨，在這間從你大學畢業之後一待就是六年的公司，面對處處提攜你的幾位前輩，你想寫一封感謝信……

Dear Mr. Smith,

I am writing this letter to let you know that I'll be leaving ABC at the end of January.

Thank you so much for your guidance and inspiration over the past six years. **It's been a pleasure working with you**, because you are not only an excellent problem solver, but also a genuine and reliable team player.

I am so grateful for the opportunity to work alongside you.

You can email me anytime at amazingserena@gmail.com or call me at 0987-654-321.

Thank you for everything.

All the best,
Serena

親愛的 Smith 先生，

我想跟您說我一月底要離開 ABC 公司。

真的非常謝謝您過去六年的提攜，與您合作無比愉快，不僅因為您是一位絕佳的解決問題者，更因為您是一位真誠可靠的團隊工作者。

我很感激能有機會與您共事。

您能透過我的電子郵件 amazingserena@gmail.com 或是手機號碼 0987-654-321 聯繫到我。

再次感謝您。

祝福您，
Serena

實用例句應用指南

各種讚美

❶ Thank you for making our work life much easier and happier.
謝謝您讓我們每天的工作更順利、更快樂。

❷ **You are a great pleasure to work with.**
跟您工作相當愉快。

❸ You are not only my co-worker, but also a great friend that I trust.
在公司裡面你不只是我的同事，也是一個我信任的好朋友。

❹ **You've accomplished so much** and we're going to miss your guidance and positive attitude.
您一路走來實踐了非常多，我們會想念您以及您正面積極的態度。

❺ **If it weren't for you,** I wouldn't have known that confidence is contagious. I will never forget how you inspired and mobilized everyone in our team.
如果不是你，我不會知道原來自信是會傳染的。我將不會忘記你是如何激勵與動員我們的團隊。

對退休人士的祝福與讚美

❻ Happy Retirement! Enjoy fabulous quality time with your friends and family.
退休生活愉快！盡情享受與朋友和家人歡度的時光。

❼ Your contributions to ABC will never be forgotten.
您對 ABC 公司的貢獻不會被淡忘。

對退休人士的幽默祝福

❽ No more meetings and no more KPIs[1]. Enjoy your new chapter in life!

不用再開會了，連 KPI 都沒有囉！好好享受你人生新的篇章！

---

❾ You made it! **All your hard work has paid off! I wish you a wonderful retirement**.

你做到了！你努力的一切終於有回報了！祝福你退休生活愉快。

---

❿ Congratulations! **From now on** every day is a holiday!

恭喜！現在開始每一天都是你的假期了！

離職相關例句

⓫ It's been a pleasure working with you. I will never forget your kindness, guidance, and support.

與您共事是我的榮幸。我不會忘記您的善良、指導以及支持。

⓬ I will be moving to Paris in two months due to family circumstances. Christina Cho, our senior sales representative, will **take over as manager after my departure**.

因為家庭因素，我將在兩個月內搬到巴黎。我們的資深業務代表，Christina Cho，將會在我離職後接掌經理一職。

⓭ You have my full commitment to ensuring a smooth transition.

我承諾會協助讓交接順利。

---

[1]KPI：Key Performance Indicators 關鍵績效指標

慣用語與句型應用指南

❶ It's a pleasure / It's my pleasure / my pleasure
我的榮幸；（客氣）哪裡哪裡

▶ A：It's very kind of you to give us a lift.
謝謝你順道載我們一程。

B：Oh, **it's a pleasure**.
哪裡哪裡。

"It's a pleasure to..."

用來表達「to 後面的整件事情」是一件很榮幸、喜悅的事情。

▶ **It's a pleasure** to meet you.
很榮幸認識你。

❷ If it were not for...
如果不是……（某某事情就不會發生）

▶ **If it weren't for** your donations, we wouldn't have succeeded.
如果不是您的捐款，我們不會成功。

單字片語應用指南

❶ collegial　同事之間的（相處融洽的氣氛與關係）

▶ The office has a welcoming **collegial** atmosphere.
這間辦公室內部相處融洽，讓人感到備受歡迎。

❷ demanding　（形容某人事物）耗費精力時間的

▶ I don't think I could cope with this **demanding** job ever.
我不覺得我有辦法再做這份如此操勞的工作了。

❸ genuine （東西是）真正的、名符其實的
（人／感情是）真誠的、真心的

▶ I decided to forgive her because her apology seemed **genuine**.
我決定原諒她，因為她的道歉似乎是真心的。

▶ Smith is a humble, **genuine** person.
Smith 是個謙虛、真誠的人。

❹ tons (informal) 很大的數量（非正式用法）

▶ We have **tons of** work to do.
我們有超多工作要做。

❺ regardless of 即使；不管

▶ He still did it **regardless of** the risk.
他不顧危險還是做了那件事情。

▶ They are willing to support us **regardless of** our mistakes.
即使我們犯了錯，他們還是願意支持我們。

❻ retirement 退休

▶ The age of **retirement** for all employees is 65.
所有員工的退休年齡是六十五歲。

▶ His psychiatrist suggested that he take early **retirement**.
他的心理醫生建議他提早退休比較好。

❼ spirit 精神；意志

▶ You always lift our **spirits**, even in demanding situations.
即使在最辛苦的時候，你總是能夠鼓舞大家。

★ team spirit 團隊精神

★ in a spirit of cooperation 合作的精神

LETTER **17**

Thank You for Your Hard Work & Congratulations on Your Promotion

感謝你的努力 & 恭喜升遷

對於下屬的精彩表現給予感謝並且讚揚，對於獲得升遷肯定的同事或是客戶給予恭賀祝福，這一封滿滿喜悅與肯定的信件，除了 "Congratulations（恭喜）" 之外還有什麼方式可以參考呢？

 小建議大思考 Suggestions

❶ 不要浮誇

段落精簡、用字清晰最為恰當，過多美言的用語反而顯得浮誇而不真誠。

❷ 不要失焦

信件目的是恭賀，記得主角是對方。如果你想要提及工作往來的事情，還是另擬一封信件比較好，別讓這封祝賀信失焦。

 書信寫作步驟 Step by Step

#給下屬的激勵信

STEP 1　表達感謝重視對方的付出

I would like to thank you for bringing out the best in our team.

謝謝你幫助展現出我們團隊最好的一面。

STEP 2　提及對方實際的貢獻

I am pleased to inform you that the Vice President is exceedingly satisfied with the X-Plus project. Thank you for the amazing work you've done for our team and it is worthy of special recognition.

我很高興通知你，副總非常滿意我們的 X-Plus 專案，謝謝你優異的工作表現，你的付出值得特別嘉許。

STEP 3　鼓勵並且再次感謝

Thank you for your hard work.

感謝你的努力。

 情 境 A Situation A

Andrew 是你下屬，你注意到他最近在專案管理上表現良好，想藉此機會寫一封簡短的嘉許信給他，對他的努力表示肯定。

 範 例 Example

Hi Andrew,

Thank you for your hard work, commitment, and innovative ideas. We are pleased to inform you that the Vice President is exceedingly satisfied with the X-Plus project. Thank you for the amazing work you've done for our team and it is worthy of special recognition.

We are truly appreciative of your efforts and dedication.

Look forward to our next project.

Warm Regards,
Serena

親愛的 Andrew，

謝謝你的努力、全心投入及創新的想法。我們很高興地告訴你，副總非常滿意 X-Plus 的專案表現，謝謝你優異的工作表現，你的努力值得特別的嘉許。

我們非常謝謝你的貢獻與心力。

期待我們下一個合作專案。

祝好，
Serena

#恭喜同事升遷

STEP 1　先恭喜再說

Congratulations on your new appointment as product manager.
恭喜你，晉升產品經理新職。

STEP 2　感謝對方的付出及讚美對方的優點

Thank you for always stepping up when deadlines loom.
謝謝你總是在截止日逼近的時候挺身而出。

STEP 3 再次恭喜給予祝福

You have our full support. Congratulations.
我們支持你。恭喜你。

 **情 境 B** Situation B

Andrew 原本是跟你同一個部門的同事,他最近升遷到其他部門,你想寫信告訴他,你為他的成就感到開心,也謝謝之前的合作默契。

 範 例 Example

Hi Andrew,

Congratulations on your new appointment as product manager. It is a well-deserved promotion.

Thanks so much for always stepping up when deadlines loom. You go above and beyond to help achieve our team's goals. You have made us all proud. We will miss you here.

Keep up the good work. Congratulations!

All the best,
Serena

嗨 Andrew，

恭喜你，晉升產品經理新職，實至名歸。

謝謝你在截止日邊緣總是挺身而出，你超乎我們期待的協助完成團隊目標，你讓我們感到驕傲，我們會想你的。

繼續保持亮眼，再次恭喜！

祝好，
Serena

#恭喜客戶升遷

（步驟同情境 B）

 情 境 C Situation C

早上你看到長期合作的美國客戶 Andrew 發了一則 Twitter "Happy to announce I am the new Product Manager. #promoted #newchapter （很開心告訴大家我是新任產品經理囉！ #升遷 #新篇章）" 你知道他等這個認可已經兩三年了，你非常為他高興，但是你突然一下子覺得腦袋一片空白，除了「恭喜你，這真的是個天大的好消息」之外還能說些什麼呢？

Hi Andrew,

I'd like to send you our warmest congratulations on your promotion. All the sacrifices that you have made paid off.

You not only do everything in your power to finish your tasks but also go above and beyond to help achieve your company's vision. I can't think of anyone else who deserves this recognition more than you do.

Congratulations and keep breaking your own records! Onward and upward!

All the best,
Serena

嗨，Andrew，

我由衷為您的升遷感到高興。你一路走來的犧牲付出在此刻得到報償。

你不只是盡全力把分內事務完成，更超乎期待地協助達成貴公司的願景。我想不出除了你之外還有誰值得這份肯定。

恭喜並請繼續打破你的紀錄！一路長紅！

祝好，
Serena

❶ **Congratulations on** this wonderful recognition of your merits.
我帶著莫大的喜悅向你祝賀，恭喜你升遷。

❷ Congratulations on your new position/appointment as product manager at Jason & Amilia.
恭喜你在 Jason&Amilia 公司的產品經理新職。

❸ **Please send her** my congratulations, **together with** my best wishes for the happiness of her family in the coming year.
請代我恭賀她，也祝福她的家人在新的一年愉快。

❹ It gives me great pleasure to extend my warmest congratulations to you on your new role/success/achievement.
我為您感到高興，向您致以最熱烈的祝賀，恭賀您的新角色／成功／成就。

❺ I was thrilled when I heard about your well-deserved promotion through Twitter.
我從 Twitter 上面知道你升遷的好消息，為你感到非常高興。

❻ A person like you always **stands out from** the crowd. I am so happy for your success.
茫茫人海，你是那個總是脫穎而出的人，為你的成功感到高興。

❼ **Keep up the good work**.
繼續保持亮眼。

❽ **You have made us all proud**.
你讓我們感到無比驕傲。

❾ We wish you all the best in your future endeavors.
希望你未來一切順利。

⓾ Keep breaking your own records! Congratulations!

繼續再創佳績吧！恭喜你！

⓫ **Good luck in** your new job.

新工作祝你好運。

慣用語與句型應用指南

❶ It gives me great pleasure...　我很高興……

★搭配動詞用：great, deep, enormous，表示「非常」

▶ **It gives me great pleasure** to welcome our guest speaker today.

很高興來歡迎我們今天的主講人。

❷ go above and beyond　做得遠超乎大家的期望、期待
（例如職責之外、分內之外的事情）

▶ The police officer **went above and beyond** the call of duty.

這個警察做得超乎大家的期待。（雖非分內之事）

❸ keep up the good work　（稱讚）繼續保持好的表現

▶ My mom told me if I **keep up the good work**, she would raise my allowance.

我媽媽告訴我如果我繼續保持好的表現，她會增加我的零用錢。

❹ onwards and upwards　步步高升；越來越成功

▶ Congratulations. Your business is moving **onwards and upwards**.

恭喜，你的生意蒸蒸日上。

▶ If you want to be successful, you must have ambition to move **onwards and upwards**.

如果你想成功，你必須有企圖心要一步一步往上爬。

❺ stand out from the crowd

在人群中脫穎而出（與一般人明顯不同或相當引人注意）

▶ Be yourself and you can **stand out from the crowd**.
做你自己，你可以在人群中脫穎而出。

單字片語應用指南

❶ deserve　值得；應得

▶ You **deserve** it after all your hard work.
在如此努力付出之後，這是你應得的（獎賞、獎勵等等）。

deserved　（形容詞）值得的

▶ It is a well-**deserved** victory.
這是當之無愧的勝利。

❷ hooray　表達開心；鼓舞

▶ Hip, hip, **hooray**!
耶～耶～萬歲！

▶ **Hooray**! I won!
喔耶！我贏了！

❸ merit　優點；價值

▶ We have to assess the **merits** of both proposals before making our decision.
在做決策之前，我們必須清楚兩個提案的優點。

on one's own merits　根據本身的特點來判斷、評斷

▶ The board will judge all applicants on their own **merits**.
董事會將會根據所有申請者自身特點條件為基礎來斟酌的評斷。

❹ payoff / result / reward　成果；結果

▶ All you have to do is work hard and there will be a big **payoff** in the end.
你需要做的就是努力工作，最後會有好結果的。

❺ pay off　取得成功；得到好結果

▶ All your hard work will **pay off** in the end.
你辛勤工作最後將會得到報償／會有好結果。

---

❻ recognition　認可；賞識；表揚

▶ My coworker complained that the firm never gave him any **recognition** for his work.
我同事抱怨事務所從未讚賞他的工作表現。

▶ Jane finally was presented with an award in **recognition** of her years as director of finance.
Jane 終於獲獎，以表彰她多年來擔任財務總監一職所付出的心血。

---

❼ sacrifice　犧牲（時間、金錢、健康等）

★搭配動詞要用 make。

▶ We appreciate all the **sacrifices** you made for this community.
我們感謝你為了這個社區所做的犧牲奉獻。

獻祭（宗教等儀式）

★搭配動詞要用 perform、offer，意思是把某物當成祭品。

▶ Food and wine are offered as **sacrifices** to the gods.
食物跟酒用作為獻給神的祭品。

Condolence Letter to Colleagues/Clients

給同事／客戶悼念的慰問信

商務往來的慰問信函最主要的核心有兩個重點：「關懷」與「提供協助」。無論是即時給予情感上的支持，或是實質上的業務幫助，都有利於維繫彼此的商務情誼。

💬 小建議大思考 Suggestions

#提供幫助

信件除了關心，可以思考一下你實質上能提供什麼幫忙，與其只是說 "If there is anything I can do, just let me know.（如果有什麼我能幫上忙的地方，儘管開口。）" 不如更主動把願意協助的工作事務說清楚，反而更有意義。

#DoingorBeing #SabinaNawaz

哈佛商業評論（Harvard Business Review）網站專欄作家 Sabina Nawaz 用這兩個字 "Doing（有所作為）" 或 " Being（陪在身邊）" 來說明如何支持沈浸哀傷當中的同事：「一般來說，關照沈浸哀慟中的同事有兩種方式，有所作為或是陪在旁邊，他們兩種都需要。（Broadly speaking, there are two ways you can support a grieving colleague: doing or being. Mourners need both.）」

📧 書信寫作步驟 Step by Step

STEP 1 開門見山致哀

On behalf of all employees/personnel of ABC, we **extend our deepest sympathies** to you and your family during this difficult time.

謹代表 ABC 全體員工，在這個艱難的時刻，我們向您致上最深的哀悼之意。

STEP 2 緬懷死者（如果沒有交集或特殊事蹟則可以省略）

Dr. Nelson's friendly spirits and generosity endeared him to us all. We mourn the incalculable/immeasurable/sad loss along with you.

Nelson 醫師善良大度的性格讓他備受愛戴，我們與你一同哀悼如此巨大的哀傷。

STEP 3 提供幫助

❶ 一般禮貌說法：

We know that this is a difficult time for you and your family. If we may help you to lighten your load in any way, please let us know.

現在對你與你的家人來說必定是十分煎熬的時刻，如果我們能提供什麼協助來減輕你的哀傷萬分之一，請讓我們知道。

❷ 更直接的說法：

If you have any questions or concerns, like additional/extra/more time off or a flexible schedule, please let me know.

如果你有任何問題，像是延長休假或是彈性工時，請讓我知道。

STEP 4 慰問短句結尾

▶ You are in our thoughts.
我們念著您。

▶ Our deepest condolences
我們最深切的悼念

▶ Our deepest sympathies go out to you and your family.
給予您與您的家人，我們致上深切的慰問。

▶ Our heartfelt condolences to your family
向您的家人致哀

▶ With heartfelt sympathy
由衷哀悼

 情 境 Situation

你在 ABC 公司擔任行銷部門的主管，今天早上你收到團隊成員 Tim Smith 的來信，他的父親，鼎鼎大名的 Nelson 醫師，在晨間運動的時候心臟病發驟逝，你要以部門的名義寫一封慰問信給 Tim，你該怎麼寫呢？

 範 例 Example

Dear Tim,

We here at ABC were truly sorry to hear of the loss of your father. Please allow me, on behalf of all of us at ABC, to extend my sincerest sympathies to you and your family as you struggle through this period of grief.

We know that this is a difficult time for you and your family so we are here to help in any way we can, and Miss Huang, my secretary, will be contacting you shortly to see what we can do for you.

If you have any questions or concerns, like additional time off or flexible schedules, please let me know.

You are in our thoughts.

Sincerely,
Serena

親愛的 Tim，

我們在 ABC 聽聞您父親去世的消息都感到非常哀傷。在您與您的家人正承受無比傷痛的時刻，我謹代表 ABC 全體向您以及您的家人，致上最深切的慰問之意。

我們知道這些日子您與家人一定會很辛苦，我們會盡力協助您度過，我的秘書，黃小姐會與您聯繫看看是否有任何我們可以提供協助的地方。

如果你有任何問題或是擔憂，像是延長請假，或是彈性工作時間等，請讓我知道。

我們掛念著你。

誠摯地，
Serena

員工家屬過世

❶ All of us at ABC are deeply saddened by the sudden passing of Dr. Nelson. Please accept our deepest/sincerest condolences.
獲悉 Nelson 醫師驟然離世的消息，ABC 公司全體上下都感到非常難過。請接收我們最深切／誠摯的慰問。

❷ Dr. Nelson's **positive attitude and philanthropic endeavors** inspired the participation of others.
Nelson 醫師積極奮發的態度以及對慈善事業的熱情感染了所有人。

❸ Although words seem woefully inadequate/empty/superfluous in this difficult time, please know that you and your family are in our thoughts.
雖然此刻或許多說無益（不足／徒勞／多餘），我還是想讓你知道，我們掛念著您與您的家人。

公司內部公布消息

❹ **It is with great sadness** that I write to inform you that Nelson Smith, senior manager at ABC, died yesterday morning, July 27th, at National Taiwan University Hospital.
很哀傷的告訴您這個消息，Nelson Smith，我們 ABC 公司的資深經理，昨天早上（7 月 27 日）於台灣大學附設醫院過世了。

❺ I am sorry to announce that our product manager, Nelson Smith, passed away last night.
很遺憾通知您，我們的產品經理，Nelson Smith，昨天晚上過世了。

❻ **We received very sad news concerning** Nelson Smith, our marketing consultant, among the passengers on the Puyuma Express train that crashed yesterday.
我們方才獲悉行銷顧問 Nelson Smith 是昨天事故的普悠瑪列車上的乘客之一。

❼ We are deeply shocked and saddened by the tragic loss of our faithful friend.

我們失去了一位忠實的朋友，感到震驚與萬分傷感。

❽ **Our hearts go out to** Nelson Smith, whose mother passed away in a tragic accident.

我們的心與 Nelson Smith 同在，他的母親在一場意外當中過世了。

慣用語與句型應用指南

❶ **extend/offer your sympathy/sympathies**
告訴失去至親的某人，你感到很遺憾

★ **extend** 指的是「給予 (offer)」的意思

▶ I would like to **extend** my thanks to you for your kindness.
對於您的善意我由衷的感謝。

▶ The CEO **extended** a warm welcome to the guest speaker.
總裁給予講者熱烈的歡迎。

★ **sympathy** （名詞）同情

★ **sympathize** （動詞）同情；憐憫；體諒

▶ She is very kind and thoughtful and she always **sympathizes** with people in trouble.
她很善良又體貼，她總會同情遇到困頓的人們。

❷ **It's with great sadness that...**　非常悲傷的是……

▶ **It's with great sadness that** my dog passed away last night.
非常悲傷的是我的狗昨天過世了。

❸ I/we announce the passing of... 我／我們要告訴大家……過世

▶ With great sadness, **I announce the passing of** our beloved manager.
很悲傷的是，我要告訴大家我們敬愛的經理過世了。

❹ I/we must inform you of the passing of...
我／我們必須告訴大家……過世

▶ I **must inform you of the passing of** our major investor.
我必須告訴大家我們主要的投資者過世了。

❺ I/we inform you that... 我／我們要通知您……

▶ I **must inform you that** the company is considering downsizing the staffs.
我必須告訴大家公司正在考慮裁員。

單字片語應用指南

❶ endear sb to sb 使……受到……的歡迎與喜愛

▶ The couple **endeared** themselves **to** the whole town.
這對夫妻讓整個城鎮的人都愛他們。

▶ The singer's talent has **endeared** her **to** the public.
這個歌手的才華讓她備受大眾喜愛。

❷ flexible schedule/working 彈性的（可變動的）工作時間

▶ **Flexible schedules** could be the key to reduce the friction between work and life that affects many more women than men.
相較於男性，工作跟生活之間的矛盾對女性更加困擾，彈性工作時間可能是減少摩擦的關鍵。

❸ lighten your sorrow / make your situation easier
緩減、減輕悲傷；讓情況好過點

▶ We will do anything to **lighten your sorrow**.
我們會盡全力減輕你的傷痛。

❹ on behalf of　代表

▶ He wrote the condolence letter **on behalf of** his department.
他代表整個部門撰寫這封慰問信。

❺ sadden　讓人傷心難過

▶ It **saddens** me to think that I will never see you again.
一想到再也見不到你，我就感到傷心。

▶ I am deeply **saddened** by this tragedy.
這個悲劇讓我們深陷哀傷當中。

❻ woefully　（情況）非常糟糕

▶ Medical supplies here are **woefully** inadequate.
這邊的醫療資源嚴重的不足。

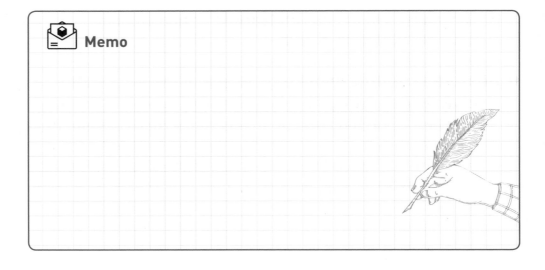

Memo

LETTER ⑲

Wedding Congratulations
新婚誌喜

西方國家對於婚禮的習俗多有不同，祝賀新人的禮物與卡片是很常見的方式，而卡片上需要寫些什麼呢？像是 "You guys are made for each other（你們是天生一對）"、"You found the other half / your soulmate（你找到了靈魂伴侶）" 都是很受歡迎的句子，不過也有許多人提倡與其用上述字詞過度浪漫美化婚姻，不如實際一點強調這是一段攜手成長度過考驗的旅程（journey）。因此，本帖也提供除了單純浪漫之外的實用例句，讓讀者自行斟酌使用。

 小提醒大領悟 Reminders

❶ 別只把卡片上面印好的句子再抄一遍

換句話說，盡量掌握句型自己修改，不要原封不動使用本帖的模板句子，不然有時候會讓人覺得好像是賀年卡模板大集合。祝賀信或卡片的真正亮點，應該還是你跟新人之間的情感才是。

❷ 切忌拖拉

盡量在你得知好消息的「當下」馬上著手寫信，會讓對方感受到你也因為這個喜訊而感到萬分高興。

書信寫作步驟 Step by Step

STEP 1 恭喜恭喜

Congrats, Sandra and Alistair! It's so great to see two awesome people like you getting married!

恭喜 Sandra and Alistair！看到像你們倆這麼讚的人結為夫妻真的是太棒了！

STEP 2 感謝新人

It means so much for me to be a part of your big day/ special day!

謝謝你讓我參與這個屬於你的特別日子，對我來說意義重大！

STEP 3 提及彼此共同的美好回憶

You two are the most humorous and sweet people I have ever met. May you always make each other laugh!

你們倆根本是我見過最幽默貼心的人，願你與她繼續讓彼此歡笑下去吧！

STEP 4 溫暖的結語

這部分跟商務正式結尾所去不遠，如果新人是你很熟很親的朋友，你也可以用幽默風趣的方式表達，請參考範例後面的實用例句應用指南。

It's official! Wishing you a life full of happiness, love, and adventures.

這是來真的囉！祝福你們展開充滿歡笑和愛的旅程。

情 境 Situation

你明天要去參加外國好友 Alistair 的婚禮，但是恭喜他們新婚的卡片還是空白的，你想寫一段又溫馨又有意義的賀喜短箋⋯⋯

範 例 Example

Congrats, Sandra and Alistair!

It's so great to see two awesome people like you getting married. Thank you for letting me share such a joyful and blessed day with you. I'm so overjoyed for both of you.

You two are the most humorous and sweet people I have ever met. May you always make each other laugh.

Wishing you a life full of happiness, loved adventures.

Here's to a long and happy marriage!

Lots of love,
Serena

Sandra 跟 Alistair，恭喜你們！

好開心看到兩個這麼棒的人結為連理。謝謝你們讓我見證美好賜福的這一天，我好為你們感到高興。

你們兩位簡直是我遇過最有幽默感、最貼心的人，希望你們以後一直讓彼此開懷大笑。

祝福你們展開充滿歡笑和愛的旅程。

敬一段綿長快樂的婚姻！

很愛很愛你們，
Serena

實用例句應用指南

❶ **Couldn't be happier for you**! Love you both!
為你感到超級高興！愛你們！

❷ So happy for you guys, **you are perfect for each other**!
太為你們高興了，你們是天生一對！

❸ **May the happiness you feel today last forever.**
希望你今天所感受到的愛與喜悅能永永遠遠。

❹ **We're thrilled to be celebrating** your special day with you!
我們非常開心能跟你一起慶祝這特別的一天！

❺ **Thank you for letting us** share such a joyful and blessed day with you.
謝謝你讓我們分享你的喜悅。

❻ Thanks for inviting us to eat and drink. **Happy wedding day**.
謝謝你邀請我們來你的婚禮吃吃喝喝～結婚快樂。

❼ Congratulations on finding your **one and only partner in crime**.
恭喜你找到唯一的死黨了。

❽ Here's to a long and happy marriage!
敬長久喜樂的婚姻！

如果你寫新婚賀卡的對象是姻親，可以多加入以下用語在 **STEP 3** 的位置，讓賀卡更顯溫馨。

❿ So glad to have you both as part of our bigger family!
我們是一家人了，太開心了！

⓫ Sandra, welcome to our small but crazy family! Hugs and kisses.
Sandra，歡迎你加入我們這個小但瘋狂的家庭！抱抱親親。

⓬ Sandra, **you've been like family** for a long time, but now **it's official.**
Sandra，你一直以來就像是家人一樣了，不過現在是正式來囉！

慣用語與句型應用指南

❶ Here's to... （宴席上）請眾人一起舉杯給予某人、某事祝福
"make a toast to someone or something"

▶ **Here's to** the happy couple! May they find great happiness together.
敬快樂的佳偶！願他們共築歡笑。

▶ **Here's to** love and friendship!
敬愛與友誼！

▶ **Here's to** Monica and Chandler!
敬 Monica 跟 Chandler！

❷ Couldn't be happier 非常快樂的意思
▶ **Couldn't be happier** for you.
我為你感到非常高興。

Couldn't be worse/better 形容人、事、物最糟或最好也不過如此。
▶ My relationship **couldn't be worse/better**.
我的感情很糟／很不錯。

❸ We're thrilled 我們非常激動、興奮
▶ She **was thrilled to death** about her promotion.
她對於升官這件事情感到非常興奮。

★ **thrilled to death/pieces** 加上 "death/pieces" 加強語氣。
▶ **I was thrilled** to hear that they got married.
聽到他們結婚了，我感到非常興奮。

單字片語應用指南

❶ blessing （神）賜福；喜事；幸運的事
▶ It's a **blessing** that we all survived the accident.
我們都能在意外當中生還，真是萬幸。
▶ My daughter is a **blessing** to me.
我的女兒是上天賜給我的福氣。

❷ congratulations 恭喜；恭賀
★要以複數形式呈現。
▶ **Congratulations** on your wedding.
新婚恭喜。

❸ overjoyed （通常在聽到好消息後）極為高興的
▶ "While introverts are no less likely to feel enthusiastic than their more outgoing colleagues, they tend to express it in subtler ways. 'That means that when your team has a

victory, the introverts may not appear to be as **overjoyed** as everybody else,' Cain says."

—TIME

「雖然內向的人比起比較外向的同事並非就比較少能感受到熱情，但是他們傾向用比較不明顯的方式表達情緒，『比如說當你的團隊獲得勝利，內向的人看起來就不像其他人表現的那樣興奮。』Cain 說。」

— 《時代雜誌》

❹ **partner in crime** 　一起胡鬧的好兄弟、好姐妹、好麻吉

▶ Happy birthday to my BFF (best friend forever) and my **partner in crime**.
祝福我最好的朋友、好麻吉生日快樂。

💬 **娜娜老師告訴你小趣聞** ────────

The reason why wedding dresses are white.
婚紗是白色的緣由。

從什麼時候開始，新娘都是穿白色禮服呢？這要從英國女王維多莉亞（Queen Victoria）說起。距今 178 年前，維多莉亞女王選擇在自己的新婚之日穿上白色絲緞蕾絲禮服，然而在當時，紅色才是普遍新娘禮服的顏色。

而 "**white wedding**" 這個字也是從新娘禮服的白色而來，代表傳統在教堂舉行新娘以白色裝束的婚禮形式。

另外 "**shotgun wedding**" 是形容婚禮以非常迅速的方式安排進行，因為女生已經有孕在身，也是奉子成婚之意。

From Baby Shower Wishes to Newborn Baby Congratulations

祝福即將有新生兒、恭喜獲得新生兒

迎接新生兒是闔家歡樂的大喜事，除了 "Congratulations" 這個字之外，還有許多令人感動的表達方式。

 小提醒大領悟 Reminders

---

❶ 小心你寫的賀詞會被大聲唸出來

一般 "baby shower（迎接新生兒的派對）" 會有拆禮物時間，換言之，你的卡片很有機會被大聲朗讀出來，所以要注意一下，不要寫太私密的話題。

❷ 除了 Dear 還可以怎麼開頭

招呼語有許多溫馨用法可以替換，當然 "Dear 某某某" 是不會有錯的，或者也可以用逗趣的方式 "To the most fabulous **mommy-to-be**（給最棒的準媽咪）"

此外，如果你收到的 baby shower 派對邀請函署名是準媽媽跟準爸爸一起敬邀，那你的賀卡稱呼就應該寫「夫妻的名字」。或者，你也可以用寫給準媽媽肚子裡的「寶寶的名義」來祝福你的好友及她即將出世的寶貝。

❸ 簡潔有力最貼心

新手爸媽可是忙得焦頭爛額，沒空仔細閱讀長篇大論喔！

 書信寫作步驟 Step by Step

#寶寶還沒出生

STEP 1 溫馨道賀祝福

Congratulations on the upcoming arrival of your **little one**.
恭喜小寶寶要誕生囉！

STEP 2 祝福

It means so much to be here with you today. You're going to be an amazing mom! **I wish nothing but** happiness and success for you both.
好開心今天能與你分享你的喜悅，你一定會是一個超讚的媽媽！我祝福你開心沒有煩惱，母子平安順利。

STEP 3 好字祝福結尾

▶ Overjoyed 欣喜若狂地

▶ Over the moon 好開心

▶ Lots of Love 滿滿的愛

▶ All my love 滿滿的愛

▶ Blessings 祝福

▶ Happy snuggling 抱抱愉快

你的好友 Daniela 即將臨盆，她在家裡舉辦 Baby Shower，你受邀參加，正在抉擇要送 diaper genie（尿布桶）還是 baby milestone blanket（寶寶成長紀錄毯），同時也苦惱著賀卡上面應該寫什麼，好表達你的祝賀之情……

 範 例 Example

Dear little one,

I can't wait to see you and hug you. I'm sure you'll have your mommy's beautiful eyes. You should see how excited she is. She is the sweetest person I have ever met. You're gonna have the best mommy in the world.

Welcome to the world, little one!

See you soon,
Serena

親愛的小寶寶，

我等不及要見到你了，好想抱一抱你呀！我說你一定會有跟你媽咪一樣漂亮的眼睛，你真應該看看她有多興奮。她是我見過最貼心的人了，你會有一個全世界最讚的媽媽。

歡迎來到這個世界，小孩！

很快見到你，
Serena

#寶寶已經出生

STEP 1 恭喜恭喜

❶ **對新生兒的父母**

▶ So happy for you two! You are going to make amazing parents.
真為你們高興！你們倆一定是超讚的爸媽。

❷ **對寶寶**

▶ Welcome to the world! So thrilled that you're here!
歡迎來到這個世界！我好開心你來了！

STEP 2 關心新手爸媽，關心小寶寶或是進一步提供幫助

I can't wait to help you with the little one. If you need anything, just let me know.
等不及要幫忙你照顧小寶寶了，如果你需要任何幫忙，儘管跟我說！

STEP 3 溫暖結語（別忘了把你的另一半或親近熟識的家人的祝福，一併帶進賀卡裡）

▶ My wife/husband/partner/[name] also sends her/his best wishes.
我的老婆／先生／伴侶／[名字] 也要祝福你們的新生活愉快。

▶ Much love to you 很多的愛
▶ Lots of love 很多的愛
▶ Sweet dreams 美夢
▶ Rock-a-bye 乖乖睡

Daniela 跟 Fraser 在上個月迎接他們期待已久的小寶寶,他們在生產前舉辦的 baby shower,你因為人在台灣沒有辦法親自參與。如今,你收到新手爸媽傳來的溫馨合照以及興奮喜悅的訊息,身為好友的你,想要寫一封賀卡,表達你的祝福。

 範 例 Example

Dear Daniela and Fraser,

Congratulations on the arrival of your little princess. So happy for you two! You are going to make amazing parents. My partner also sends her best wishes. Have a wonderful time with the little one.

Lots of love,
Serena

親愛的 Daniela 跟 Fraser,

由衷祝賀你們的小公主誕生了。好為你們夫妻高興!你們一定會是最棒的父母。我的伴侶也為你們感到無比高興。育兒生活順利愉快。

很多的愛,
Serena

❶ Congratulations to the best parents the world could ever hope for.
恭喜兩位，全世界夢寐以求的最棒父母。

❷ Warmest/Heartiest congratulations on the birth of your sweet baby girl/boy!
獻上最溫暖的祝福給你的小寶寶！

❸ Cutest baby is on the way. Enjoy all these precious moments!
最可愛的寶寶就要來囉，盡情享受珍貴的每一刻！

❹ To the magic of motherhood!
敬神奇的母愛！

❺ Welcome to the world! I'm looking forward to being a part of your life.
歡迎來到這個世界！我好期待參與你的成長。

❻ Sometimes the smallest things take up the most room in your heart.

—Winnie the Pooh

有時候最小的事情能佔據你的心。

—小熊維尼

❼ Wishing you a lifetime of happiness, laughter, and joy.
祝你一生幸福快樂。

❽ Have a wonderful time with the little one. I know you will be the best dad/mom.
育兒生活愉快，我知道你一定會是最棒的爸爸／媽媽。

假設妊娠期間母親受了不少苦，或是新生兒剛出生的時候有一些狀況，可以多增加這樣的句子：

❾ **So thankful** your sweet little baby is here. A warm welcome to precious baby and lots of love to amazing mom.
無比感激你的寶寶來到人世。溫暖的問候給寶貝孩子，滿滿的愛給最棒的媽媽。

慣用語與句型應用指南

❶ **I wish nothing but...** 除了⋯⋯以外，都不要；完全⋯⋯
  ▶ Give me **nothing but** Coke.
     給我可樂，其餘免談。
  ▶ She is **nothing but** smart.
     她超聰明的。
  ▶ I wish **nothing but** happiness for you.
     我只希望你快快樂樂。

❷ **anything but...** 除了⋯⋯之外都可以；一點也不⋯⋯
  ▶ Give me **anything but** Coke.
     給我除了可樂以外的飲料。
  ▶ She is **anything but** smart.
     她一點也不聰明。

❸ **be over the moon** 非常高興的意思
  ▶ Amy **was over the moon** about/with her birthday presents.
     Amy 收到生日禮物非常開心。

❹ **Wishing you...** 祝福你⋯⋯
  ▶ I/We **wish you** a happy holiday.
     我們祝福你佳節愉快。
  ▶ **Wishing you** a happy holiday.
     祝福你佳節愉快。

★ 記得 wish 放句首要加 ing，Wish you a happy holiday 是錯的喔！

❶ little one (informal)　小孩子

▶ I really enjoed playing with my sister's **little one** last weekend.
我真的很享受上週末跟我姊姊的小孩玩的時光。

❷ mommy-to-be　準媽咪

to-be 字尾意指不久的將來，同理很常見的像是：bride-to-be（準新娘）

▶ It feels like we were in the university yesterday, and today you are the **mommy-to-be**! Time flies!
我們在大學的時光就向昨日一樣，而今天你就是準媽媽了！時光飛逝！

❸ on the way　在路上；就要發生

▶ They have 2 kids and another **on the way**.
他們就快要有第三個小孩了。

❹ Rock-a-bye　一首唱給小孩聽的美國晚安曲

▶ **Rock-a-bye Baby**, on the tree top　嬰兒搖搖，在樹梢

When the winds blows, the cradle will rock　風兒吹，搖籃晃

When the bough breaks, the cradle will fall　樹枝斷，搖籃墜

Down will come baby, cradle and all　寶寶搖籃墜落地

❺ tickled pink (informal)　非常高興（非正式用法）

▶ We were **tickled pink** to be invited.
我們很高興被邀請。

▶ She asked me to marry her. I'm **tickled pink**.
她要我跟她結婚，我好開心。

★ **in the pink** 意思不同，意思是某人身體健康。

▶ My grandmother was ill for a month, but she's **in the pink** now.
我奶奶病了一個月了，但是她現在狀況很好。

❻ upcoming 即將到來的；即將發生的

▶ I can't go out with you guys, I need to prepare for my **upcoming** exam.
我不能跟你們大家出去，我必須為即將到來的考試做準備。

❼ xoxo (informal) 流行用語，意思 **hugs and kisses** 親吻跟擁抱

▶ Lots of love, **xoxo**
很多的愛，親親抱抱

💬 **娜娜老師告訴你小趣聞**

What is Baby Shower?
Baby Shower 是什麼？

在維多莉亞時期，當時女性懷孕會很低調守密，直到臨盆母子均安，女性友人就會舉辦下午茶會來祝福新手媽媽以及新生兒。現在的 baby shower 則是在臨盆之前舉辦，baby shower 本來都只有女性受邀，而且通常會是已經生產過的女性，不過現在也有許多人舉辦這樣的派對，親朋好友都受邀，也不會只限於女性友人。

LETTER ㉑

A Letter of Condolence to Friends
給朋友悼念的慰問信

當你的親友正經歷至親至愛離去的痛苦，你或許身在遠方不能親身前往致哀，或是考量到對方在治喪期間，你不願意過度打擾，但仍想表達你的關懷之情。這時，一封溫柔體貼的弔唁信能夠適切表達你的支持。本帖的架構與最後的範例是比較長的書信篇幅，假設你使用社群媒體與對方聯繫，**STEP 1** 可以先快速簡短傳達慰問遺憾之情（參考 **STEP 1** 及實用例句應用指南），再透過電話或書信，仔細慎重的把關懷之意傳達給對方。否則，一句 "I am sorry for your loss" 或是 "RIP"，在現今網路浮濫的世界，都顯得空泛沒有溫度。

此外，如果是「隨花束附上的小卡片」，可以參考更多實用例句應用指南簡短搭配。

 小提醒大領悟 Reminders

避免說大道理

中文習慣用「節哀順變」這四個字表達哀悼之意，原意是請喪家節制哀傷，順應親人驟逝的變故。用英文表達哀悼之意很常見的是："I am sorry for your loss"，這個 "sorry" 不能翻作抱歉，而是「很遺憾」，我們可以發現這兩種語言傳遞關懷的角度不太一樣：中文很習慣用勸慰的方式，例如：

▶ Be strong.
你要堅強。

▶ He is free now. His suffering has ended.
他的病痛已經結束了，他自由了。

▶ At least she's no longer suffering.
至少她已經脫離苦痛了。

▶ Everything happens for a reason.
事情的發生都有其理由。

這些通常都不太適合用在英文弔唁信裡，與其「勸慰」，英語母語使用者較常透過「緬懷」以及「讚頌」死者，來表達關懷慰問。

#Sincerity #EmilyPost

身為一位社交禮儀大師，也是《近代美國禮儀文化》一書的作者 Emily Post 強調「一封弔唁信可能是相當生硬、結構不夠工整的，不符合文法規則的，沒關係，文辭的優雅在這裡並不重要，真誠才是這封信最重要的價值。」（A letter of condolences may be abrupt, badly constructed, ungrammatical—never mind. Grace of expression counts for nothing; sincerity alone is of value.）

 書信寫作步驟 Step by Step

STEP 1　表達深感遺憾與致上慰問心意

I am sorry for your loss. **My thoughts go out to** you and your family.
我很遺憾你痛失摯愛，向你與你的家人致上慰問。

STEP 2　讓信件內容細膩並且貼近人心（視熟識程度而定）

The thing I will miss the most is those inspiring conversations your mother and I had. I will also miss her beautiful smile that always lit up the room when she walked in.

我最懷念的莫過於與你母親那些激勵人心的談話，我還會想念她美麗的微笑，她所到之處，都是目光的焦點。

STEP 3　提供幫助

If you'd like, I can come by this week and bring a dish / I can bring dinner over tomorrow night. Please let me know if there is anything else I can do to help.

如果你願意的話，我這個禮拜去拜訪你／我明天晚上可以帶晚餐過去。請讓我知道任何有我能幫得上忙的地方。

STEP 4　慰問跟祝福

We are missing your mother along with you. You are in our thoughts and prayers.

我們與你一起緬懷想念你的母親。我們與你同在。

 情　境 Situation

你的英國朋友 Nancy 的母親不久前過世了，你無法親身到告別式，撥電話也覺得唐突，你想透過一封信表示關懷，該怎麼寫呢？

Dear Nancy,

I am so sorry for your loss. My heart goes out to you.

I remember at your graduation party your mother's whole face lit up whenever she talked about you. She was so proud of you. I feel so lucky that I got to know her. What a remarkable life! I admired her selfless devotion to those people in need. I'll always cherish those beautiful moments with her. The thing I will miss the most is those Sunday chats we shared together. Nobody could tell funny but inspirational stories like your mom. She will be deeply missed.

I am sorry that I couldn't fly to the UK but I am keeping you in my thoughts and prayers during this difficult time. You know I will always be there for you.

My love and sympathy to you and your family,

Serena

親愛的 Nancy，

我感到非常遺憾。我與你同在。

我還記得在你的畢業派對上，你母親一談到你就神采飛揚，她是如此為你驕傲。我有幸能認識你母親，她活出如此非凡的一生！我景仰她無私豐沛的奉獻，對所有需要幫助的人伸出援手。我永遠珍惜與她共度的美好時光，其中我最為懷念的就是那些週日閒談，我沒見過誰能像你母親這樣，把故事說得又好笑又啟發人心。她會永懷我們心中。

我很抱歉我不能飛到英國去看你，但是在這個艱難的時刻，我念著你，我的心與你同在。你知道的，我一直都在。

慰問你與你的家人，

Serena

❶ I am thinking of you during this difficult time. My heart goes out to you.

在這個痛苦的時刻，我念著你，我與你同在。

❷ Our thoughts (and prayers) are with you and your entire family.

我們的愛（和祈禱）與你和你的家人同在。

❸ **It saddened me** to hear from Jason that you had lost your mother. My thoughts are with you in this difficult time.

從傑森那邊得知你母親過世的消息，我感到很哀傷。在這艱難的時刻，我與你同在。

❹ It was truly a pleasure working with your mother for 3 years. She was so warm and humorous that she could magically lift our spirits. **She will be deeply missed**.

有幸與你的母親共事三年，她是如此溫暖又風趣，能神奇的振奮人心。她會長存我們心中。

❺ What a thoughtful and generous man your grandfather was. I'm grateful that I got to know him. His positive attitude and wisdom inspired me, and I will always miss him.

你的祖父如此體貼大度，我能認識他，備感榮幸。他的正向態度以及智慧一直都鼓舞著我，我將永遠懷念他。

❻ What an extraordinary life! **It's an honor to have known** your father/mother. He/She was such a sweet and kind gentleman/lady and I will always remember him/her.

如此非凡的一生！我如此有幸能認識您的父親／母親，這樣一位貼心寬和的紳士／女士，我會永遠懷念他／她。

❼ Although I never met Mr./Mrs./Ms./Miss [family name of a person], I **will never forget how much your eyes lit up** when you talked about him/her.

即使我從未見過 [姓氏] 先生／夫人／女士／小姐，我不會忘記你每次談到他／她時，你的眼睛都在發亮。

❽ Please let us know if there's something we can do to possibly comfort you a little bit: bringing over meals or running errands. We just want to let you know you won't go through this alone.

有任何我們能做的，能讓你稍微好過一點，請務必告訴我們，帶食物過去或處理生活大小事。我們只是要讓你知道，你不會獨自一人面對這一切。

❾ **Whatever you need it will be done**. We will always be there for you.

無論你需要什麼，儘管開口。我們隨時都在。

❿ I hope you feel surrounded by much love of family and friends. We love you.

我希望你能感受到你被許多親友的愛包圍著。我們愛你。

如果你是喪家，收到慰問之後，可以參考以下簡短的句子表達感謝：

❶ Thank you for your kindness / kind offers.

謝謝您的善意。

❷ **Thank you for your support during this difficult time**.

謝謝您在這段艱難的時間給我們支持。

❸ Thank you for your loving/warm/sweet/kind message.

謝謝您充滿愛／溫暖／親切／體貼的訊息。

❹ The flowers you sent in honor of my grandmother were so beautiful. We appreciate your kindness and thoughtfulness.

您送來獻給我祖母的花束真美。我們感激您的善意跟體貼。

❺ Thank you for sending the beautiful wreath to the funeral home. We are grateful to have friends like you in our lives. Thanks for everything.

謝謝您送到殯儀館來的美麗花圈，我們很感激生命中能有您這樣的好友。謝謝您所做的一切。

慣用語與句型應用指南

❶ find comfort in...　從……得到慰藉

中文句子裡面，得到慰藉的「得到」就可以用 find 來表達。

▶ May you **find** peace and **comfort in** the love of your family.
願意你在家人的愛當中得到安慰。

❷ I am (so) sorry to...　我對於……感到遺憾；難過

▶ I am **sorry to** hear you didn't get the job you want.
我對於你沒有得到你想要的工作感到遺憾。

小心，不要跟道歉用語 "sorry about that" 搞混。

▶ I totally forgot it. **Sorry about that**.
我完全忘記了，真不好意思。

❸ If you would like...　你想……的話；你願意……的話

信件當中你所提出的幫忙，應當都算是請求，所以會用 would 來表達請求之意。

▶ I can do the household chores for you while you are suffering from the broken arm **if you would** like.
如果你願意的話，在你手臂斷掉這段期間，我可以幫你做家事。

❹ Our/My thoughts and prayers are with you.

用 "thoughts and prayers" 來表達哀悼十分常見，像是：

▶ We send **our thoughts and prayers** to the victims and their families.
我們的心與受害者及其親友同在。

❺ someone's heart goes out to another.
某人向某人表達憐憫傷懷之心。

▶ Our **hearts go out to** the victims and their families.
我們為受害者及其家屬感到心痛不捨。

單字片語應用指南

❶ appreciate... 感激……

▶ I **appreciate** your kindness.
我感謝你的好。

欣賞；讚賞

▶ My boss **appreciates** my work.
我老闆欣賞我的表現。

❷ be proud of someone 為某人的成就感到驕傲、欣慰

很常用於父母子女之間，像是：

▶ Your father must **be** very **proud of** you.
你的父親一定為你感到無比驕傲。

如果這位父親已經不在人世，動詞時態以「過去式」來表達：

▶ Your father **was** so **proud of** you, and he lit up whenever he spoke about you.
你的父親如此為你感到驕傲，他無論何時提到你總是神采飛揚。

❸ come by 順道拜訪；短暫停留

▶ She said she'd **come by** later.
她說她等一下會過來。

▶ They **came by** after dinner.
他們晚餐之後有來找我。

❹ condolence　**悲傷、悼念；與某人同感哀傷、哀悼**

▶ a letter of **condolence**
弔唁信

▶ They came to offer their **condolences**.
他們前來弔唁。（通常用複數型）

❺ get to know　**逐漸熟悉、了解**

▶ You just need a few weeks to **get to know** our new system.
你需要花幾週時間來搞懂我們的新系統。

▶ He seems to be nice. I would like to **get to know** him.
他看起來人不錯，我會想多認識了解他。

❻ go through something　**經歷；承受**

▶ I am sorry that you have to **go through** this all alone.
我很抱歉你必須獨自走過這一切。

仔細查看；檢查

▶ We will **go through** your documents and get back to you soon.
我們會仔細看過你的文件之後再聯繫你。

❼ light up　**（人）展露笑顏；高興起來。**

▶ Her whole face **lights up** when she talks about her daughter.
當她談到女兒，一臉笑意。

▶ His eyes **lit up** when his wife walked into the room.
當他老婆走進來的時候，他眼神亮了起來。

❽ privileged
享有特權、特殊利益的

▶ They had **privileged** access to the files.
他們有讀取這些檔案的特權。

榮幸

▶ I feel **privileged** to meet her.
我對於認識她感到很榮幸。

因為這個「認識的緣分」是他人無法獲得的機會，表示非常珍貴。

❾ remember...
記住……

▶ Please **remember** your promise.
請記住你的承諾。

記得；印象

▶ Do you **remember** me?
你記得我嗎？

▶ I **remembered** the first time I met you.
我記得我第一次認識你的時候。

代為問候

▶ Please **remember** me to your family.
請代我向你的家人問好。

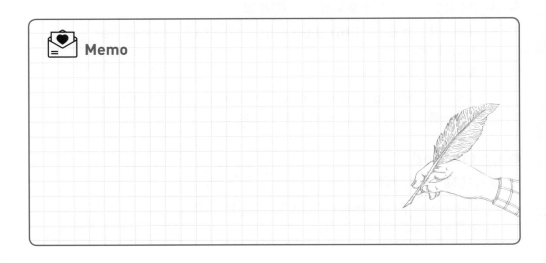

Memo

Thank You for Always Being There for Me

謝謝你一直都在

琑碎日常的小事分開來看都沒什麼大不了，以至於我們很容易遺忘，忘記好好感謝身邊那個「從沒離開過」的朋友。找個機會把謝謝說得令人難忘吧！讓這些人知道，因為有他們，你覺得自己是多麼的幸運。

 小提醒大領悟 Reminders

寫這帖沒有什麼禁忌，只有一件事情提醒常常過於委婉或是惜字如金的人，肉麻是無上限的，讓看信息的對方被你肉麻到又哭又笑的，正是本封信的目的。勇敢又有創意的把你的感謝說出來吧！

 書信寫作步驟 Step by Step

STEP 1　問候

Hey, my favorite person in the world, how have you been? **I miss seeing you.**

嘿，這個世界上我最喜歡的人，你好嗎？好想你喔！

STEP 2　表達心中感謝

Thank you for being there for me **through thick and thin**. You gave me hope in life's most difficult situations and it means a lot to me.

謝謝你一直都在。你在我最艱難的時候給我希望，這對我來說意義深重。

STEP 3　關心對方近況

▶ How's your new job going? You must be exhausted for the big presentation coming up. It's amazing that you always stay positive and never lose your sense of humor. I believe that you will definitely nail it.

你的新工作如何呢？你最近一定為了那個大簡報累死了吧！你真的好棒，總是那麼正面，還能保持你的幽默感，我相信你一定會表現得超讚的。

▶ **I'll keep my fingers crossed for you**.

我會幫你祈禱的。

STEP 4　閒話家常以及溫馨關懷

Take care of yourself and keep **living life to the full**. Don't forget to share photos on Instagram.

好好照顧自己，盡情活出你的人生。記得要在 Instagram 上多發點照片。

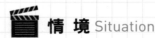 **情 境** Situation

你在英國讀書的時候認識了 Jenny，這麼多年來 Jenny 總是給你最中肯的建議，在你遇到低潮時，也是他告訴你應該相信自己。聖誕假期將至，你想藉此問候他並且說出你的感謝……

Hi! My favorite person in the world,

I haven't seen you in ages. How have you been?

Do you remember that I hit rock bottom because I didn't get the scholarship? You told me that if the plan doesn't work, change the plan, not the goal. Thank you for always supporting and encouraging me. Thank you for standing by my side **through thick and thin**. My dear friend, you bring out the best in me.

Glad to hear that you nailed the interview. So proud of you. How's your new job going? I would love to hear more about your new job.

Take care of yourself and keep **living life to the full**. I miss you and I wish you all the best.

Lots of love,
Serena

嗨！這個世界上我最喜歡的人，

超久沒見了，你都好嗎？

還記得嗎？當時我沒申請到獎學金，我的心情低落到谷底。你告訴我，如果計畫失靈，就改變計畫，而不是改變目標。謝謝你一路支持我、鼓舞我，謝謝你陪我度過人生的低潮。我親愛的朋友，你幫助我展現最好的自己。

好開心你搞定了面試，為你感到驕傲。新工作如何呢？想聽你的分享。

好好照顧自己，盡情享受每一天。我很想念你，祝福你一切順利。

滿滿的愛，
Serena

感人說友情

❶ A true friend is someone who is there for you when he'd rather be anywhere else.

—Len Wein

真正的朋友是即使他寧願去別的地方，他卻仍待在你身邊。

—蘭‧偉恩

❷ Good friends like you come along once in a lifetime.
如你一般的好朋友一生只會遇到一次。

❸ **I haven't seen you in/for ages. I miss seeing you.**
距離上次見面已經好久以前了，我很想念你。

❹ Thank you for listening to my complaints and not just judging me.
謝謝你總是聽我抱怨並且不會去論斷我。

❺ Thank you for listening to my complaints about those things you probably had no idea of.
謝謝你總是聽我抱怨那些你根本不想聽的事情。

幽默說友情

❻ Friendship is born at that moment when one person says to another, 'What! You too? I thought I was the only one.'

— C.S. Lewis

友情誕生在當其中一個人跟對方說，「什麼，你也是？我還以為只有我這樣」。

— C.S. 路易斯

❼ **Thank you for being my biggest fan.**
謝謝你作為我的頭號粉絲。

雞皮疙瘩說友情

❽ Growing up with you is **the best thing that ever happened to me**.
跟你一起長大是發生在我身上最美好的事情。

❾ Thank you for loving me for exactly who I am.
謝謝你愛我，因為我是我。

❿ Thank you for understanding me like no one else does.
謝謝你如此了解我，無人能及。

⓫ Thank you for **making my ordinary life extraordinary**.
謝謝你讓我平凡的人生不同凡響。

⓬ Thank you for being you.
謝謝你是你。

慣用語與句型應用指南

❶ keep one's fingers crossed / cross one's fingers
替對方祝福祈禱有好結果

▶ Let's **keep** our **fingers crossed**.
我們一起來祈求好運。

❷ live life to the full/fullest　盡情活出你的人生

▶ My grandmother, who inspired me the most, **lived life to the fullest**.
啟發我最多的外婆，一生活得精彩盡興。

❸ the best thing that ever happened to me
發生在我身上最好的事情

▶ Meeting you is **the best thing that ever happened to me**.
認識你是發生在我身上最好的事情。

❹ through thick and thin　不離不棄度過艱難的時刻。

▶ My partner stood by me **through thick and thin**.
我的伴侶一路走來一直都在。

❺ stand by someone　持續支持、陪伴、鼓勵某人

▶ **Stand by** me and have faith in me.
支持我，相信我。

單字片語應用指南

❶ ages / a long time　很長時間

▶ We haven't seen each other in **ages**. Miss you so much.
我們超久沒見面了，很想你。

❷ come along　到達；出現

▶ Don't worry. I will **come along** later.
別擔心，我隨後就到。

娜娜老師告訴你小趣聞

Have you heard of "Friendsgiving"?
你有聽過 "Friendsgiving" 這個字嗎？

"Friends" 加上 "Thanksgiving"，從字面上可以想像就是一群朋友聚在一起慶祝感恩節。這個字據說一開始是用來形容一群無法回家過節的大學生或是工作人士，在感恩節的時候聚在一起烤一隻火雞，一起準備配菜團聚過節。不過後來有許多人也會開始舉辦所謂的 "Friendsgiving party"，通常舉辦的時間會在實際的感恩節之前，目的當然就是聯繫感情以及慶祝友情。

Thank You So Much for Everything
一切都非常感謝你

除了「謝謝」兩個字，還有什麼說法可以表達內心的感激之情呢？那個支持你、幫助過你，在你急難的時候拉你一把的朋友，跟他／她說聲特別的謝謝吧！

小提醒大領悟 Reminders

別小看手寫卡片的力量，尤其在現代資訊轟炸的人際網路中，當你在一堆廣告信件當中發現一張友人寄來的手寫賀卡或是旅遊途中的明信片，那是有溫度的問候。

書信寫作步驟 Step by Step

STEP 1　開門大謝

I appreciate your guidance that helped me to navigate my way through difficult times.

我相當感激你給我的提攜，幫助我走過艱苦的時刻。

STEP 2　再深刻一點

You are such a compassionate friend and you inspire me a lot because of everything you do for me and for others.

你是這樣一個富有同情心的朋友，你對我以及他人的付出，深深鼓舞了我。

STEP 3 祝福對方

Keep spreading your laughter around, because I know firsthand how special it is.

繼續散播你的笑聲，因為我知道那有多特別。

 情 境 Situation

你在英國讀碩士，一轉眼就要尾聲，即將收拾行李回台灣了。你回想過去一年，受到許多人的幫助跟支持，以後也不一定有機會再相聚了，你想要對幾個朋友道謝⋯⋯

 範 例 Example

Dear Sonal,

I just wanted to take a moment to thank you for all the support you've given me when I was experiencing hard times, particularly during crazy midterms. Thank you for being so nice and thoughtful. You are such a compassionate friend and you inspired me a lot because of everything you did for me and for others.

I want to wish you all the best and I believe you will achieve your goal, because I have never met any other person with the same determination that you have.

Keep spreading your unique sense of humor, because I know firsthand how marvelous it is.

Lots of love,
Serena

親愛的 Sonal，

我想謝謝你這一年給我的支持跟鼓勵，特別是在恐怖的期中考期間。謝謝你如此貼心善意。你是這樣一個富有同情心的朋友，你對我以及他人的付出深深鼓舞了我。

我祝福你一切順利，也相信你一定能達到你的目標，因為你是我見過最有決心毅力的人。

繼續散播你獨特的幽默感吧，我親自見識過，簡直妙不可言。

很多的愛，
Serena

實用例句應用指南

感謝金錢相關援助

❶ When I was at rock bottom, **you took me in. I am in your debt** for all your help.
當我到人生谷底時，你收留我。我永遠感激你給我的幫忙。

❷ Thank you for stepping in so that I could take a break and pull myself together.
謝謝你出手相助，我才能喘一口氣，振作起來。

感謝陪伴傾囊相授

❸ Thank you for being there when my health **took a turn for the worse** last year.
謝謝你在我病情惡化的時候陪在我身邊。

❹ It's so nice of you **to take me under your wing**.
你是那麼好的一個人，願意如此呵護我。

❺ Thank you for teaching me to face challenges with dignity. I am so lucky to **have you by my side**.
謝謝你讓我知道如何有尊嚴的面對挑戰，我很幸運有朋友如你。

當感激溢於言表

❻ **I owe you big-time.**
我非常感激你。

❼ **Words are no enough to describe** how grateful I am.
文字不足以表達我有多感謝你。

❽ The simplest things in life mean the most.
生活中那些最簡單的事物，最為意義深重。

稱讚對方來表示感謝

❾ **Knowing that you were swamped with your work**, I am so grateful that you spent time helping me.
我知道你其實已經忙得不可開交，你卻還是花時間在我身上，我真的很感激。

❿ Whenever I think of kindness, generosity, and compassion, your name immediately **comes to mind**.
無論何時我想到善良、慷慨、富有同情心，你的名字馬上浮現在我腦海。

慣用語與句型應用指南

❶ be appreciative of something　（人）很有鑑賞力的

▶ It's always a pleasure to have an **appreciative** audience.
能遇到有鑑賞力的觀眾是很幸運的。

對某人、某事感激的

▶ I am very **appreciative of** your support.
我很感激你的支持鼓勵。

❷ come/spring to mind （腦海）一閃而過

▶ What **comes to mind** when you see this picture?
當你看到這張照片時，你馬上想到的是？

❸ in someone's debt 非常感激

▶ I am **in** your **debt** for your support.
感激你對我的支持。

❹ pull yourself together 冷靜下來；收拾心情；振作起來

▶ It's not the end of world so **pull yourself together**.
還不是世界末日，找回你的沈著冷靜。

❺ take a turn for the worse 情況惡化；變得更糟

▶ His grade **has taken a turn for the worse** since last semester.
他的成績從上學期開始每況愈下。

❻ under one's wing
在某人的呵護、庇護、保護下；把……帶到某人的羽翼底下

▶ I was lost in desperation and my friend Amy took me **under** her **wing**.
我當時失意至極，而我的朋友 Amy 對我關懷備至。

單字片語應用指南

❶ big-time 非常的；極度的

▶ I was so frustrated for messing up **big-time**.
完全搞砸這一切，我好沮喪喔！

❷ firsthand 第一手地；直接地

▶ My grandfather has experienced the period of Martial Law **firsthand**: questioning by the policeman when he was a youngster.

我爺爺年輕時曾經歷戒嚴時期，有親身被警察審問的經驗。

---

❸ rock bottom 最低點；最不愉快；最谷底

▶ What would you do when your marriage hits **rock bottom**?

當你婚姻觸礁的時候，你會怎麼辦？

---

❹ step in 插手；介入（為了要幫助解決問題）

▶ I couldn't find anyone to **step in** so that I could catch a break.

我找不到有誰可以幫忙，讓我可以喘口氣、休息一下。

---

❺ swamp （動詞）被淹沒、覆蓋；太過大量以至於應接不暇

▶ I am **swamped** with work at the moment. Can I get back to you tomorrow?

我現在忙得不可開交，明天再回覆你好嗎？

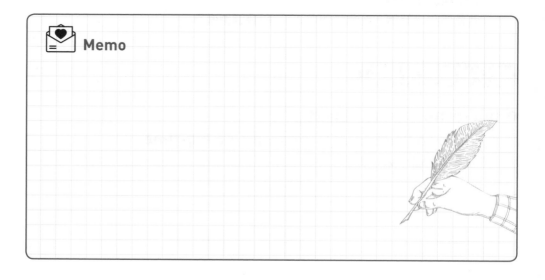

♡ Memo

LETTER 24

Thank You for Your Hospitality
謝謝你的款待

在朋友家接受款待之後,是否會想要跟朋友好好說聲謝謝呢?想想看,當他收拾完家裡,看到手機裡傳來你的溫馨感謝,心頭暖了起來。

 小提醒大領悟 Reminders

---

❶ 感動就要說出來

我們常常以為,熟識的朋友之間無須多言,但是當我們表達感激與感動,對方會感到被重視珍惜以及自我價值的提升,同時也可以避免造成只有單向付出的錯覺。如此一來,表示感謝也是一種善待對方的方式。

❷ 大寫字有律動感

例如 "You are VERY NICE" 這句話, 大寫字母 "**VERY NICE**" 就好像寫信的人大聲喊出「超讚」兩個字一樣生動,在非正式書寫溝通上表現直接。

 書信寫作步驟 Step by Step

STEP 1 直接稱謝

Thank you for your generous hospitality on my trip to Edinburgh.
這次我的愛丁堡之行受到您熱情款待,由衷感謝。

STEP 2　點出具體事實

It's very kind of you to invite me to your house. The food was divine, the place was so homey, and most importantly the host was stunning.

謝謝你邀請我去你家玩。食物似神仙般美味，家裡又整理的如此舒適，最重要的是，主人是如此光彩奪目呀！

STEP 3　期待再相會或是主動邀約

I hope you will spend some days of your summer vacation with us and I'd love to **show you around**. Look forward to having you with us next summer.

希望你這個暑假能來找我們，給我個機會帶你到處走走。我很期待下個夏天換我們招待你。

 情 境 Situation

你在英國友人 Madeline 家裡度過美好溫馨的假期，風塵僕僕回到台灣之後，想要寫一封溫暖的信感謝盛情款待⋯⋯

 範 例 Example

Dear Madeline,

I have returned home safely. Thank you so much for your loving hospitality and generosity. It's very thoughtful of you to think of me and invite me to your house. The days staying with you and your family were so warm and delightful. The food was PHENOMENAL, the place was so homey, and most importantly the host was amazingly stunning.

Oh, **the lamb was cooked to perfection**. It's truly the best that I've ever had. **I'm begging for the recipe, pretty please!** :)

Thank you for **spoiling me rotten** and **making me feel special**.

Please do come to my house next summer. We can visit some notable places like Taipei 101 and enjoy Taiwanese food.

Lots of love,
Serena

親愛的 Madeline，

我已經平安到家了，真的好謝謝你如此慷慨的款待我。你好貼心，想到要邀請我去你的家度假，與你跟你家人共度的短短幾天真的好溫暖、好快樂。你做的菜棒呆了，你的家好讚，最重要的是，主人耀眼奪目呢！

對了，你做的那道羊肉簡直完美，說真的，那是我吃過最好吃的羊肉了。跪求食譜，拜託拜託！:)

謝謝你寵愛我，讓我覺得我好特別。

夏天請一定要來我家玩。我們可以去著名的景點，像是台北 101 跟品嚐台灣美食。

很多的愛，
Serena

❶ Thank you for being such a gracious host and **spoiling us rotten**.
謝謝你這位如此親切的主人，謝謝你如此寵愛我們。

❷ What an amazing party! **Thanks for everything.**
多棒的派對呀！謝謝你所做的一切。

❸ Thank you for inviting us to the barbecue/cookout.
感謝你邀請我們參加烤肉／戶外野餐。

❹ **It was great meeting you** last weekend. You and your family are very nice.
上個週末很開心跟你們相聚，你跟你的家人都超級棒。

❺ Your beautiful chocolate fudge cake is in my refrigerator now. I look forward to eating it often throughout this summer.
你那漂亮的巧克力軟蛋糕正在我的冰箱躺著呢，我很期待這個夏天可以常常吃到它。

❻ Thank you for letting me **stay with** you last weekend and it's always great to see you all.
謝謝你邀請我到你家度週末，看到大家真的好棒。

❼ Words are powerless to express my thankfulness.
要表達我心中的感激，文字全無用武之地。

❽ I'm very lucky to have a friend like you.
我很幸運有朋友如你。

❾ **I thank you from the bottom of my heart**.
打從心底由衷的感謝你。

⑩ I'm writing to thank you for your loving hospitality and the wonderful present.
我來信感謝你的盛情款待以及美好的禮物。

⑪ Your welcoming hospitality is such a blessing.
你的真誠待客之道是天上賜福。

⑫ You made me feel so special.
你讓我覺得很特別。

⑬ Your partner's sense of humor is unforgettable. We truly enjoyed the dinner party last night.
你伴侶的幽默感令人難忘，我們真的很享受昨天的晚餐。

慣用語與句型應用指南

❶ from the bottom of someone's heart 打從某人的心底

▶ When I said I loved you, I meant it **from the bottom of** my **heart**.
我說我愛你，我是真心的。

❷ pretty please (funny way) 求求你；拜託（有趣說法）

像是小朋友一般的可愛表達方式，請求對方答應要求。

▶ Can I have one more? Please? **Pretty please**?
我可以再要一個嗎？好嗎？拜託啦？

❸ spoil someone rotten 把某人寵壞了

▶ My son is **spoiled rotten** by my parents.
我兒子都被我爸媽寵壞了。

❹ to perfection 完美

▶ The steak was cooked **to perfection**.
牛排煮得恰到好處。

❺ What a/an + [adjective] + [singular noun]
表達（情緒）配感嘆語氣

▶ **What a** sweet girl!
真是一個好貼心的女孩！

▶ **What a** surprise!
真是太驚訝了！

▶ **What a** day!
好長（累）的一天啊！

單字片語應用指南

❶ cookout　指聚會時在露天場地燒烤野餐

▶ My parents prepared the barbecue **cookout** for my brother's birthday party.
我父母為我弟弟的生日派對準備了戶外的烤肉野餐。

---

❷ divine　如神一般的；絕妙、美好、極佳的

▶ Thank you so much. The meal was just **divine**.
太感謝你了，這一餐如天堂般美味。

---

❸ show someone around　帶某人到處逛逛、參觀

▶ I **showed** my Italian friend **around** when she travelled to Taiwan.
當我義大利的朋友到台灣旅遊時，我帶她到處參觀。

---

❹ stay　暫住；逗留

▶ We usually **stay** with our grandparents for two weeks in the summer.
夏天我們通常都會去祖父母家待兩週。

---

❺ stay overnight

▶ Don't worry. You can **stay overnight** if you want to.
別擔心，如果你想的話你可以住一晚沒關係。

THANK YOU 謝謝

Idioms
好禮貌書寫慣用語

❶ get a/your foot in the door 通過門檻

❷ show someone the ropes 指導某人如何做（事情）

❸ onwards and upwards 步步高升；越來越成功

❹ stand out from the crowd
在人群中脫穎而出（與一般人明顯不同或相當引人注意）

❺ be over the moon 非常高興的意思

❻ keep one's fingers crossed
替對方祝福祈禱有好結果

❼ in someone's debt 非常感激

❽ pull yourself together
冷靜下來；收拾心情；振作起來

❾ take a turn for the worse 情況惡化；變得更糟

❿ under one's wing 在某人的呵護、庇護、保護下

⓫ pretty please 求求你；拜託

⓬ spoil someone rotten 把某人寵壞了

Part 3

SORRY 對不起

好禮貌運動
關於真心誠意「道歉」與勇敢「做自己」的大學問。

商務篇 BUSINESS

熟人篇 FRIENDS

How to Apologize to a Client
如何向客戶道歉

有員工失察、失言（put one's foot in one's mouth）或是公司商品出現瑕疵、客戶服務發生問題等等，造成客戶精神上或實質上的損害，道歉信函是請求客戶諒解的基本配備。

 小建議大思考 Suggestions

---

❶ 切勿含糊其辭

道歉信的內容需要清楚確實而非含糊其詞，讓收信的對方可以感受到你面對事實的誠意。

❷ 對不起三個字只是開始

避免讓對不起三個字變得虛應故事，如何「妥善處理後續」才是整封信的重點。

 書信寫作步驟 Step by Step

STEP 1　直接「承認」事實

▶ **I apologize for** my **off-the-cuff** remarks in our meeting this afternoon. **I should have** dealt with the situation differently.

我想為了今天下午在會議中不加思索的言行跟您說聲抱歉。我應該要換一個處理方式。

STEP 2　站在對方立場來希望對方諒解

You wanted to figure out the best solution with us, but I put you through a long time-wasting process and that's not professional.

您前來向我們尋求最好的解決方法，但我卻讓您歷經一段長時間的流程，這並不是一個專業的做事方法。

STEP 3　補償／重塑信任

We value your trust and partnership and humbly hope that you would give us a second chance.

我們重視您的信任與夥伴關係，並謙卑地希望您願意再給我們一次機會。

 情 境 Situation

你已經很多天沒有睡好，許多事迫在眉睫，讓你焦頭爛額，這天下午你還臨時被叫去跟客戶開會，席間有些爭論。當下你認為自己只是就事論事，會議結束冷靜下來之後，卻發現自己似乎有些失言。該如何寫這封信才可以好好表達歉意，而不是越描越黑呢？

 範 例 Example

Hi Miss Johnson,

I apologize for my behavior in our meeting this afternoon. I realized how insensitively outspoken and unprofessional I was. At ABC, we have been proud to help all our customers find the best solution in the most effective manner. Unfortunately, I let you down today.

I value your trust and partnership and you can rest assured that this situation will never occur again.

Thank you for your invaluable support,
Serena

Johnson 小姐您好，

我想為我下午在會議中的行為向您道歉。我意識到自己過於直言，並未展現應有的專業態度。在 ABC 公司，讓客戶能用最有效率的方法找尋到最棒的策略，一直是我們的驕傲。很不幸地，我今天讓您失望了。

我很重視您的信任與夥伴關係，請您放心，這種情況不會再發生第二次。

謝謝您的寶貴支持，
Serena

實用例句應用指南

❶ I realized **how insensitively outspoken I was** yesterday.
我發覺到我昨天真的是少一根筋又心直口快。

❷ Words cannot express how sorry I am for the frustration that you experienced.
文字不能表達我多麼為您所感受到的挫折而感到抱歉。

❸ We regret that we did not deliver on the experience we had promised to you.
對於我們並未達成對您所承諾的體驗，我們深表遺憾。

❹ **You can rest assured that this situation will never occur again**.

您可以放心，這種情況不會再發生第二次。

❺ We have set new guidelines to ensure that **this situation will never occur again**.

我們已經設立了新的工作準則以確保這種情況不會再發生第二次。

未能準時交貨

❻ **We sincerely apologize to you for** the delay in delivery of the products you ordered.

未能準時交付您訂購的產品，我們誠摯的向您致歉。

❼ We are sorry that you haven't receive the items you ordered and sincerely apologize for any inconvenience caused.

很抱歉您尚未收到您訂的物品，造成您任何不便，我們誠摯的向您致歉。

如果你是公司主管，代表公司以及造成疏失的內部人員向客戶道歉

❽ Please accept my sincere apology on behalf of our company.

謹代表敝公司向您致上最誠摯的歉意。

❾ It is painful and unfair to you that you have to experience the feelings again while you are **filing a complaint**.

當您在提出申訴時需要再經歷一次這樣的感受，對您來說是令人痛苦且不公平的。

❿ **Thank you for bringing this matter to our attention**.

謝謝您讓我們意識到問題所在。

一般動之以情道歉句

⓫ We failed to deliver on our promise and we are deeply sorry.

對於未達成我們的承諾，我們深感抱歉。

❶ subject someone to something / someone be subjected to something
使某人承受、遭受（不公正的對待）／某人被遭受到（不公正的對待）

▶ We didn't mean to **subject** you **to** such an ordeal.
我們無意讓您承受如此巨大的苦難。

▶ The lawyer revealed that his client **had been subjected to** unfair treatment.
律師發現他的客戶曾受到不公正待遇。

❷ bring the matter to someone's attention
讓某人了解問題所在

▶ Thank you so much for **bringing the matter to** my **attention**; otherwise, things would get worse.
非常感謝您讓我知道這個問題，否則事情會越演越烈。

❶ deliver　兌現；達成（承諾）

▶ If a company fails to **deliver** on their promise, it would be difficult to create customers for life.
如果一間公司無法達成他們的承諾，想要擁有忠誠的客戶是不太可能的。

❷ learn　學習；聽說；被告知；獲悉某消息

▶ We are really sorry to **learn** that your experience with our customer service was not what you expected.
得知您對於我們的客戶服務不滿意，我們深感抱歉。

❸ off-the-cuff　未經思索的

▶ Let me apologize for my **off-the-cuff** remarks.
讓我為自己不經思索就脫口而出的話語跟你道歉。

★本句摘錄歐巴馬擔任美國總統期間去信一位歷史系教授的致歉信函。

❹ on behalf of someone / on someone's behalf　代表某人

▶ Lisa accepted the award **on behalf of** the company.
Lisa 代表公司領獎。

❺ (rest/be) assured　（用於安慰某人）放心；不要擔心

▶ "**Rest assured**, little boy," said the detective.
警探說：「別擔心，小男孩。」

❻ second chance　第二次機會；改過自新

▶ Although my neighbor's attitude was rude and unreasonable, I still decided to give him a **second chance** after his apology.
雖然我鄰居的態度很粗魯又無理，我還是決定在他道歉之後，再給他一次機會。

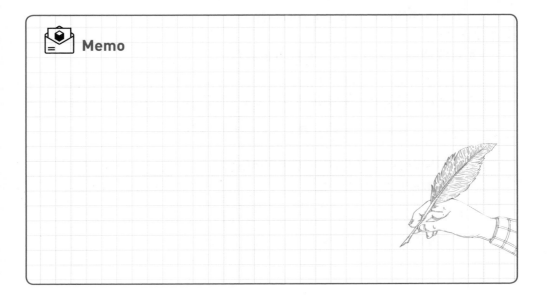

📧 **Memo**

Sorry for the Delayed Response
抱歉太晚回覆

無論是什麼原因，若我們稍晚回覆對方的訊息或信件，基於禮貌都會在回信的起頭表達抱歉之意。不過，道歉字句其實只是面對造成對方久候的不便，更重要的關鍵內容還是對方當初來信的目的是否可以被解決。

 小建議大思考 Suggestions

---

❶ 遲做總比不做好（Better late than never）

面對自己太晚回覆對方的窘境，加以解釋並且妥善回覆對方的需求，對夥伴關係的經營有長遠正面的影響。

❷ 有些情境「感謝」比「道歉」更適合

到底是否需要「道歉（I apologize...）」呢？視情況而定。比如說對方是來信問候而已，你或許隔了一兩週之後才回覆，信件開頭與其用「道歉」，不如直接「感謝」對方來信問候更適合。

▶ Thank you for your message.
謝謝您來信問候。

▶ Thanks so much for your kind note last month!
很謝謝您上個月的問候！

書信寫作步驟 Step by Step

STEP 1 道歉

Please accept my sincere apologies for the delay in responding to your request.

對於延遲回覆您的信件，向您致上誠摯的歉意。

STEP 2 解釋（視情況跳過，直接轉正題）

Emails are answered on a **first-come, first-served basis**.

我們依照收到信件的順序來逐一回覆。

STEP 3 信件正題、解決問題

Your order should arrive within 5 business days.

您的訂貨會在五個工作天內送達。

STEP 4 安撫感謝

Please let me know if that suits your need. I would love to help if you have any concerns.

請讓我知道這有沒有符合您的需求。如果還有任何疑慮的話，我很樂意幫忙。

情 境 Situation

客戶來信想要確認他所訂購貨物的交期，同一時間你發現工廠生產出了狀況，但是延遲交貨的時間也尚未確認，你決定等確認更新的交貨日期再一併回覆，但得到工廠通知預計完成日時，已經是好幾天後了……

範 例 Example

Dear Miss Morrison,

I apologize for not responding to your email sooner. My response has been delayed due to the fact that our supplier failed to deliver the products on time.

The shipment is now rescheduled for delivery on November 30th.

Thank you very much for your patience. It has been a pleasure to serve you. Please let me know if you have any questions related to your order.

Sincerely,
Serena

親愛的 Morrison 小姐，

很抱歉不能早一點回覆您。這是因為我們的供應商未能準時交貨。

您的貨物會重新安排在 11 月 30 日出貨。

非常謝謝您的耐心，很榮幸能夠為您服務。若有任何關於訂單的問題，請隨時聯繫我。

誠摯地，
Serena

實用例句應用指南

❶ I am sorry for the delayed response.
抱歉太晚回覆您。

❷ My apologies for not **getting back to you** about your request sooner.
沒有早一點回覆您的詢問，向您說聲抱歉。

❸ We are sorry that it took longer than we estimated/ expected.
我們很抱歉時間比預估／預期的還長。

❹ I regret to inform you that we have not been able to solve the problem in time.
很遺憾的要通知您，我們尚無法在期限之內找到解決方法。

因為忙碌所以晚回覆

❺ **Please accept my apologies for the delay in responding to** your information request. Things have been crazy here lately.
我最近這邊事情一團混亂，很抱歉這麼晚才回覆您的詢問。

❻ I **didn't mean to** take so long but I have been so busy doing...
我不是有意要拖延這麼久，但是我忙於……

慣用語與句型應用指南

❶ **I didn't mean to...** 我不是有意／故意這麼做……

▶ I **didn't mean to** hurt you.
我不是有意要傷害你。

單字片語應用指南

❶ take long 花很久時間

▶ Don't worry. I won't **take long**.
別擔心，我不會花太長時間。

❷ get back to someone 回覆某人（電話、郵件等）

▶ The customer service representative promised me that she would **get back to** me as soon as possible.
客服人員答應我說她會儘快回我電話。

❸ ever since 從某個時間點以後一直

▶ Anna has been frustrated and negative **ever since** she got fired.
自從 Anna 被解雇之後，心情一直很低落沮喪。

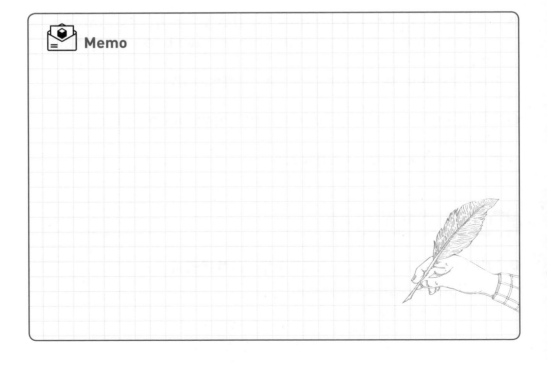

Memo

How to Reject Candidates with Grace
如何婉拒應徵者

告知應試者未被錄取的消息，從當下的時間點來看或許頂多是個禮貌動作，但是以長遠角度來看，今日認為不適合的應徵者，未來或許有機會成為有助於公司成長的關鍵人物。要讓你的潛在人才庫（candidate pool）越活力充沛，這封「未錄取通知信」也扮演了關鍵角色。

 小建議大思考 Suggestions

---

❶ 未來再聯絡
拒絕今日的面試者，不代表你就必須「切斷與對方的商務關係（sever ties with them）」。

❷ 拒絕信也代表公司
應試者或許非常喜愛你們的公司品牌，甚至是品牌產品的支持者。換句話說，未錄取通知信也是彰顯公司品牌形象的好時機。

 書信寫作步驟 Step by Step

STEP 1　感謝對方

We appreciate that you took the time to meet with our team last Friday. It was a pleasure meeting you.
上星期五謝謝您撥冗來與我們團隊面談，很高興認識您。

STEP 2 告知結果（委婉）

We were impressed with your experience and potentials, but **we regret to inform you that** your candidacy didn't **make it to the next round**.

雖然我們對於您的經驗以及潛力感到印象深刻，但是很遺憾的要通知您，您並未獲選進入下一個階段面試。

STEP 3 再度致謝或展望未來

However, we think you're a remarkable culture fit to our company and strongly encourage you to apply for other positions in the marketing department. We wish you all the best in your future endeavors.

然而，我們認為您跟我們公司文化相當契合，我們鼓勵您來應徵行銷部門的其他職位。祝福您未來一切好運順利。

 情 境 Situation

你是一名行銷經理，最近在面試行銷專員，其中一位面試者令你印象深刻，雖然才剛從大學畢業，但是他對於公司的產品如數家珍，肯定在面試前做足了功課，他也展現對行銷職務的絕佳熱誠。可惜的是，在多方考量之後，你決定錄取另一位更有經驗的人員，最終還是必須拒絕他的申請……

Hi Jim,

We appreciate that you took the time to meet with us last Friday. It was a pleasure having you here for the interview.

As competition for jobs at ABC is usually intense, we have to make difficult decisions. While we enjoyed our conversation, we have decided to select another candidate with more hands-on project management experience. We would like to thank you for giving us the opportunity to learn about your passion and experience.

We will be posting more positions in the marketing department and I hope you don't mind if we reach out to you in the future.

We wish you good luck with your ongoing job search and your future endeavors.

Best Regards,
Serena

Jim 你好，

上星期五謝謝您撥冗來與我們面談，邀請您來面試是相當愉快的經驗。

因為 ABC 公司的職位競爭都非常激烈，我們必須在眾多出色的應徵者當中做出很困難的抉擇。雖然我們談得很愉快，但是我們已經決定要錄用另一位較有管理實務經驗的應徵者。謝謝您給我們這個機會對您的專業與熱情有更多了解。

最近我們會有更多行銷部門的職缺釋出，如果您不介意，（若有適合的職缺）我們會聯繫您。

預祝您求職以及未來諸事一切順利。

祝 好，
Serena

❶ It was a pleasure having you here for the interview.
邀請您來面試是我們的榮幸。

❷ Thank you for your interest in the position.
謝謝您對於這個職位的興趣。

❸ Although **we have decided to move forward with another candidate** for this role, we would like to thank you for coming for the interview and giving us the opportunity to learn about your experience.
雖然我們選擇了其他的應徵者，還是謝謝您前來面試，以及讓我們有機會了解您的經歷。

❹ **After much deliberation, we regret to inform you that** you have not been selected for the second interview.
經過反覆考慮，很遺憾要通知你，你並未獲選進入第二階段面試。

❺ We appreciate your interest in ABC and for the time and effort you invested in applying for this position.
感謝您對 ABC 公司的熱誠以及您為了應徵此職位所投入的時間與努力。

❻ Thank you for your patience while we reviewed all candidates' files.
感謝您耐心等待我們審核完所有面試人員的檔案。

❼ While we certainly have no doubt about your skills and professional experience, **after careful deliberation**, we have decided to go with another partner for this campaign.
雖然我們對你的技能以及專業背景毫無問題，但是經過仔細權衡之後，我們決定這個專案會跟另外一個夥伴合作。

❽ Thank you again for your interest in our company. Please accept my good wishes for your future success.
再次感謝您對我們公司的熱誠，請接受我對您未來成功的祝福。

❾ We encourage you to continue visiting our website and applying for advertised positions in the future.

我們希望您可以持續關注我們網站的徵才資訊，日後歡迎再次前來應試。

❿ We will **keep your resume on file** for future openings.

我們會把您的履歷保留在我們的資料庫以供未來的其他職缺。

慣用語與句型應用指南

❶ I wish all the best for your future endeavors.
祝你未來一切好運。

這是「道別」及「祝福好運」的常用句，endeavors 指的是嘗試努力去進行某事之意，用在這個常用句裡面泛指從此以後諸事大吉大利。簡短一點也可以說 "Good luck in your future endeavors."。

▶ Thank you for coming to the interviews, **I wish all the best for your future endeavors**.

謝謝您前來面試，我祝您未來一切好運。

❷ sever connection/links/relationship/ties with someone　切斷與某人的聯繫／連結／關係

▶ The politician has **severed** his **ties with** lobbyists for the tobacco industry.

這位政治人物已經切斷了與那些替菸草公司遊說的說客的關係。

❸ take the time　花費力氣去做某事

▶ They didn't even **take the time** to get to know who you are.

他們根本沒有花時間／心力去了解真正的你。

❶ cultural fit （商務情境中）融入公司文化。

▶ One of the most important reasons for asking open-ended questions in a job interview is to assess a candidate's **cultural fit**.

面試中詢問應徵者開放性問題的其中一個重要原因，就是要評估他是否符合與公司文化相契合。

❷ deliberation 考慮；討論

▶ After careful **deliberation**, we decided to accept the offer.

經過審慎考慮之後，我們決定接受這個報價。

❸ short list （獲獎、獲得職位等）決選名單

▶ We have created a **short list** for the job.

我們已經選出這個職位的最後名單。

▶ You are on the **short list** for the prize.

你在這個獎項的最終決選名單上。

📧 **Memo**

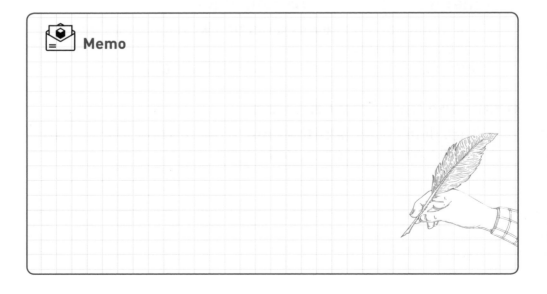

How to Gracefully Decline a Job Offer

如何婉拒一個工作邀約

面試求職的路上，可能會面臨同時有一個以上的工作機會向你招手，在你決定接下其中一份工作之後，對於其他工作機會應當給予妥善回覆，畢竟世界很小，繞了一大圈之後是否有再度合作機會都很難說，這封信是個好時機展現自己的禮貌、專業態度與誠意。

 小建議大思考 Suggestions

#把「謝謝」說得實際一點

與其空泛地說「感謝給我這個機會」，倒不如確切提及：

❶ 這間公司有哪些你欣賞的地方。
❷ 你面試的主管有無讓你欽佩的地方。

這些描述都會讓這封拒絕信發揮「人際網路」的功能。

書信寫作步驟 Step by Step

STEP 1　道謝可以更貼近人心

Thank you so much for offering me the opportunity to work at ABC.

謝謝您給我這個機會在 ABC 工作。

STEP 2　稱讚對方後，附上婉拒的理由

I sincerely enjoyed our conversations and learning about the account executive position. Unfortunately, it's not quite the right fit for my career goal.

我真心地享受我們的交談過程，並認識到關於業務執行的這個職位。很遺憾地，目前這份工作與我的職涯規劃並不是很符合。

STEP 3　再次感謝，留下聯繫資訊

Thank you again for the interview last week, and I hope our paths will cross in the near future.

再次感謝上週的面試機會，希望不久的未來有機會再見面合作。

 情 境 Situation

你一直想從事行銷相關工作，此刻同時有兩家公司寄發錄取通知給你，你選擇了一家對自己來說不僅交通便利，工作內容也相當符合期待的公司，但是你覺得對於另一家 ABC 公司感到非常遺憾，因為在面試過程中，你非常欽佩那位行銷經理，你覺得應該要將這份欽佩表達出來，讓他知道……

Dear Mr. Nash,

Thank you very much for the offer to join your team. I appreciate the time you took to make sure I was a good fit and I am grateful to have been selected.

I am impressed with the company's core values and especially what you have achieved. However, after careful consideration, I regret that I have to decline your offer. This role seems to be a great opportunity, but I have decided to pursue another role that is more in line with my career goal.

Once again, thank you for your consideration, and I wish you all the best.

Warmest Regards,
Serena

親愛的 Nash 先生,

非常感謝您提供機會讓我加入您的團隊。謝謝您的寶貴時間,我也相當榮幸能雀屏中選。

我很欣賞貴公司的核心價值,更對於您締造的佳績感到欽佩。但是在謹慎思考之後,我很遺憾必須婉拒您的工作邀約,雖然此職位是一個很好的機會,但我選擇了另一份跟我的職涯目標更接近的工作。

再次感謝您的關照,祝福您一切順利。

致上溫暖的問候,
Serena

❶ **I appreciate the time you spent meeting with me** and I am amazed by your team's strengths and what you have achieved.
感謝您撥冗面試，我非常敬佩您團隊的士氣以及您所締造的佳績。

❷ I enjoyed getting to know more about the company and the role that seems to be a great opportunity.
很高興能多了解貴公司以及這個職務內容，這對我是個很棒的機會。

❸ **Unfortunately, I have to decline the offer in light of** personal reasons.
很遺憾地，因於個人考量因素，我無法接受這個邀約。

❹ Again, thank you for your thoughtfulness throughout the hiring process.
再次感謝您在此過程中的關照。

❺ **Thank you for your time and consideration**.
感謝您的寶貴時間與關照。

❻ I do appreciate both the offer and your consideration.
我非常感謝這份工作機會以及您的關照。

慣用語與句型應用指南

do [verb]...　強調 [動詞]

▶ **Do** let me know how you're getting on in your new home.
要讓我知道你住進新房子裡面情況好不好喔！

▶ I **do** love you.
我是真的愛你。

❶ cross paths (with)　遇見；相遇

▶ I **crossed paths with** a college friend on my business trip.
我在出差的時候巧遇我的大學同學。

❷ consideration　考慮；斟酌

▶ After some **consideration**, I've decided to sell my car.
在一番斟酌之後，我決定賣掉我的車子。

體察別人心情；關心別人

▶ Chris has no **consideration** for others.
Chris 毫不關心別人。

▶ Please show a little **consideration** for the neighbors.
請考慮一下鄰居的感受。

❸ fit　適合

▶ The dress **fits** you perfectly.
這件洋裝超適合你。

❹ in line with　與某人、某事一致

▶ My thought is **in line with** yours.
我跟你想的是一樣的。

❺ in light of　由於；因為
"in the light of"

▶ **In the light of** recent incidents, we have to take particular care of our personal belongings.
由於近來事件頻傳，我們要特別看好隨身物品。

LETTER ㉙

How to Say No Through Email
如何透過電子郵件說不

當你的下屬向你提出想在年下最忙的時候休假兩週的要求；當你的客戶要求你給出超過公司能提供的貨件交期；當你的長官詢問你是否可以把你已經排好的假期延後……諸如此類的情況，要如何透過書信拒絕對方是一種藝術，說不清楚不僅造成誤會，信件不斷往返更浪費彼此時間。

 小建議大思考 Suggestions

#把「拒絕信」變成解決問題的「溝通信」

拒絕信的重點除了是要清楚告訴對方「恕難從命」之外，不妨給對方「其他建議的選擇（leave the door open）」。信件重點可以從「拒絕」轉換成「你能做什麼」，這需要換位思考一下，用軟性的語言提到「我可以理解為什麼你要求如此……」，並且適度提供處理方式。如此便能將一封商業往來的拒絕信，變成積極解決問題的溝通書信。

 書信寫作步驟 Step by Step

STEP 1　招呼

We have reviewed your vacation request for the period
September 1st -10th.
我們已經看過你提出從 9 月 1 日到 10 日的休假申請。

STEP 2　拒絕

Usually, our company's busiest time of the year is in Fall and you play such a key role. I can totally understand how it can be frustrating and disappointing, but I'm afraid that I have to decline your request.

通常，我們公司一年之中最忙的時間就是在秋天，並且你在其中扮演著關鍵角色。我可以理解這對你來說有多令人沮喪及失望，但我必須拒絕你的要求。

STEP 3　進一步提出建議方案

Although we can't give you the week of September 1st off, but alternatively you could take the week of October 7th off.

雖然我們不能讓你在 9 月 1 日的那週休假，但是替代方案是你可以在 10 月 7 日那週排休。

 情 境 Situation

你才剛擔任行銷組長兩個月，其中一名新進組員昨天來信要求在耶誕節前一週就請特休，但是公司產品總在各大節慶前熱賣，有相當多突發狀況以及繁瑣業務需要人力，而且根據公司的休假規定，你也必須拒絕這個要求……

Hi Katie,

Thank you for asking me about taking time off before Christmas. I wish I could say yes to this but regrettably I can't, since the week before Christmas is often the busiest week of the year in our department.

I can totally understand how it can be disappointing but you will be paid double time for that weekend. Also, you will have an extra day off.

Your effort is greatly appreciated and thank you for bringing your best to work every single day. Please let me know if you want to talk more about the Christmas vacation policy.

Best Regards,
Serena

嗨 Katie，

謝謝你問我關於你想要在耶誕節前休假的事情。我希望我可以答應你，但是很遺憾我不能，因為耶誕節前一週通常是我們部門最忙的時候。

我知道這可能會讓你有點失望，不過那個週末你會獲得加倍薪資。此外，你會有多一天的休假。

感謝你每日對工作盡心盡力的付出，如果你想多加討論關於耶誕節休假的規範，請讓我知道。

祝好，
Serena

❶ We were lucky to have your proposals and we appreciated the effort and time you put into this project. However, we have decided to go with another company who better suits our current needs.

我們很幸運收到你的提案，也很感謝你對此的付出。很遺憾，我們決定與另一家公司合作這個案子，更適合我們當前的需求。

❷ I was planning to spend this week working on project A, so I won't be able to cover project B at the moment.

我本來規劃這週要做 A 專案，所以我沒有辦法在此刻又去顧及 B 專案。

❸ I would love to do [things], but unfortunately **my schedule is packed** for the following weeks. I am afraid that I have to decline this offer.

我很願意去做 [某件事情]，但是抱歉再來幾週我的行程滿檔，我恐怕必須拒絕這個邀請。

❹ That sounds like an amazing idea. However, honestly I'm not very familiar with [things], so **I wouldn't be much help**.

這個提議聽起來很棒，但是其實我並不太熟悉 [某件事情]，所以我能幫得不多。

❺ Mind if I reschedule this for Tuesday? If the suggestion was tabled at a later date, **I am happy to weigh in**.

介意我把這個會議改到星期二嗎？如果這個提議被延後討論的話，我很樂意加入。

❻ Although your proposal doesn't closely suit our current needs, we would appreciate if you kept our company in mind for future partnerships. We will get in touch if circumstances change.

即使您提供的服務並不符合我們現在的需求，我們很感謝如果您願意把我們當成未來潛在的合作夥伴，如果有任何情況變動的話，我們會聯繫您。

❶ leave the door open for… 不排除……的可能性;讓門開著

▶ The patent on the medicine has expired, which **leaves the door open for** other companies to file it.
這個藥品的專利時效過期了,這給了其他公司來申請的可能性。

leave the field open for someone
不再跟某人競爭;讓出空間、機會給對方

▶ I have decided not to apply for the job, which **left the field open for** Tim.
我決定不應徵那份工作了,這讓 Tim 的贏面更大了。

❷ My work schedule is packed/jam-packed.
我的工作滿檔;時間表排滿了。

▶ The manager's schedule is **jam-packed** with meetings.
經理的行程表已經被會議塞滿了。

❸ not much 少量的;不多的

▶ To be honest, there **isn't much** difference.
老實講,沒什麼不同。

weigh in 秤重(尤指拳擊、賽馬等比賽之前的秤重)

▶ He **weighed in** at 259 lbs. for the last fight.
他上一場比賽時體重 259 磅。

積極參與討論;辯論(發揮影響力、貢獻)

▶ All managers from five branches **weighed in** with opinions regarding the campaign for the upcoming holiday season.
五間分公司的經理加入討論,對即將到來的假期行銷方案提出意見。

Politely Decline an Invitation

禮貌地婉拒邀請

當我們收到邀請函但是無法出席，拒絕對方的好意總是有點掃興，委婉的告知對方順便祝福對方活動順利，是一個既禮貌又能維持人際情意的重要步驟。

 小建議大思考 Suggestions

#婉拒的理由

一般來說，口頭邀請比起書信邀請函來得輕鬆彈性，而若想要拒絕邀約，或許在談話的當下，有沒有「理由」可能不會是影響氣氛的主要因素，但若是回覆書信邀請函，白紙黑字很容易失去溫度。這時，若能視情況說明無法赴約的理由，會更有誠意。

 書信寫作步驟 Step by Step

STEP 1 開門見山的道謝或是恭喜道賀

Thank you for your invitation to your company's luncheon.
感謝您邀請參加貴公司的餐會。

STEP 2　婉拒出席並稍作解釋

I appreciate your kindness but I have an appointment that I can't reschedule. Otherwise, I would definitely be there for you.

感謝您的好意，但我有一個不能改期的約。否則，我一定會為了您出席支持。

STEP 3　祝對方活動順利開心，或提供其他幫助

I'm sure the event will be amazingly successful.

我相信這個活動一定會相當成功。

STEP 4　溫馨結語

Thank you again for the invitation and it means a great deal to me.

再次感謝邀請，對我來說意義重大。

🎬 **情 境** Situation

英國客戶 Madeline 與你往來許多年，彼此相當熟悉，你在前一封信件當中透露你即將在下個月前往英國參加紡織商展，沒想到 Madeline 來信邀請你參加她兒子的畢業慶祝會，你備感榮幸、受寵若驚，可惜商展的行程固定，不太可能赴約，你要寫一封有感謝、有恭喜，又點抱歉的「婉拒邀請信」……

Dear Madeline,

I am grateful that you invite me to be part of Andrew's big day. **I wish I could be there for you.**

Regrettably, I will not be able to join you because I have a prior engagement that can't be rescheduled. I hope that all goes as planned. Please congratulate Andrew for me and give my regards to everyone in attendance.

Thank you for thinking of me.

Warmest Regards,
Serena

親愛的 Madeline，

我好謝謝你邀請我參與 Andrew 的大日子。我真希望我可以出席與你們同慶。

很遺憾地，我沒辦法參與你們，因為同時間我已經有一個不能改期的約。希望慶祝會萬事順利。請幫我跟 Andrew 說聲恭喜，也祝福當天所有參加的賓客。

謝謝你想到我。

最溫暖的祝福，
Serena

❶ Thank you so much for the **invitation to** your house warming party.

謝謝你邀請我參加喬遷派對。

❷ Thank you very much for **inviting me** to your daughter's birthday party.

非常感謝你邀請我出席你女兒的生日會。

❸ **I wish I could** make it but I won't be able to celebrate it with you due to another business commitment.

我真希望我可以去，若非必須工作，一定會出席與你一同慶祝。

❹ **I regret to inform you that** I won't be able to attend owing to a prior engagement on the same day.

不好意思我無法出席，因為同時間已經有其他安排。

❺ **It sounds like** a nice tribute to Dr. Smith, but I will be out of town at the time of the event. I am sorry that I will not be able to attend.

這個活動聽起來是個向 Smith 醫師致敬的好方法，但是我那時候剛好出城了，很抱歉沒有辦法參加。

❻ I sincerely regret that, **owing to a previous engagement**, I am unable to accept your kind invitation for the luncheon to be held on Monday, August 12th .

因為同時間已經有安排，無法參加您邀請在 8 月 12 日星期一舉辦的午餐會，我感到相當遺憾。

❼ Please congratulate Andrew for me and let him know I am amazed by his achievement.

請代我祝賀 Andrew，並讓他知道我對他的成就感到很驚喜。

❽ I wish you a wonderful night celebrating your anniversary.
願你有個美好的夜晚歡度你們的週年紀念日。

❾ Please keep me updated. I would love to help out.
請讓我知道有哪些我可以幫得上忙的地方。

❿ I apologize for not being able to join you this time. However, I am willing to do anything for future events.
很抱歉這次無法參加，但是，我很樂意為了未來的活動盡一份力。

⓫ Thank you for thinking of me. This invitation means a lot.
謝謝你想到我。這份邀請函對我很重要。

慣用語與句型應用指南

❶ It sounds like... 聽起來；似乎

▶ **It sounds like** a good idea.
聽起來是個好主意。

類似用法 **as if**

▶ You looked **as if** you just did a great job!
你看起來像是你做得很好似的。

❷ If I could...I would... 如果我（當初）可以……我會……

▶ What **would you** do **if you could** do anything?
如果你可以做任何事情，你會做什麼？

❸ Please give my regards to someone.
請代我問候某人。

▶ **Please give my regards to** your parents.
請代我問候您的雙親。

❹ Please keep me updated. 請讓我知道後續更新的情況。

▶ Best wishes to your study in Edinburgh. **Please keep me updated**.
祝福你在愛丁堡的求學，請讓我知道你在後續的生活情況。

單字片語應用指南

❶ engagement 約定的會面；預約

▶ I'm afraid I have a previous **engagement**.
對不起我已經有約了。

❷ a great deal 很多

▶ Things could be **a great deal** worse.
事情有可能更糟的。

❸ reschedule 改期；重新預約

▶ The conference has been **rescheduled** for Sunday.
研討會已經被改到禮拜天舉行。

▶ He called to **reschedule** his appointment.
他打電話來改約時間。

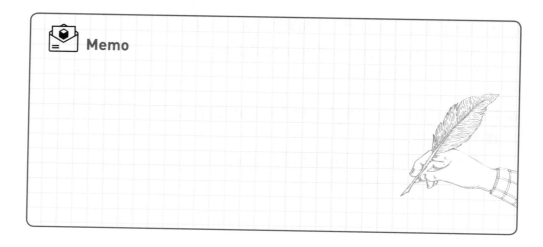

Memo

Apologize for Missing an Event
向缺席活動道歉

生活當中總會有分身乏術的時刻，即使非常想參與朋友的重大事件或聚會邀約，卻未能出席活動，讓本帖來告訴你如何把對朋友的傷害降到最低。

 小提醒大領悟 Reminders

#把話說好說滿

面對朋友的失望，除了告知對方自己不克前往之外，這封信應該還要適切表達你的遺憾與祝福。

 書信寫作步驟 Step by Step

STEP 1 為了缺席感到抱歉

I am really sorry that I am not able to attend your birthday party.
很抱歉我無法參加你的歡送會。

STEP 2　解釋為什麼缺席的理由

I was informed that I have to attend a conference in Tokyo.
我被告知要去東京參加一個研討會。

STEP 3　提出你所能做的來讓事情更好

Let's catch up when I come back.
等我回來的時候，我們聚聚吧。

STEP 4　祝福對方活動圓滿

I am sure it will be a lovely gathering and everything will be just perfect.
我相信這會是一個超棒的派對，而且每一件事情都會非常完美順利。

情 境 Situation

你的好朋友打算舉辦盛大的生日派對，因為他這一年完成了自己的夢想，又是三十大關，想要大肆慶祝，但是同時間你必須出差，這次出差是個重要的任務，你期盼最近可以有升遷機會，你不想錯過。你知道你必須選擇工作，但是同時你也希望可以讓好朋友了解你之所以缺席的理由……

Dear Jane,

So sorry that I can't attend your birthday party. It's your big day and I am so happy for you. I wish I could be there for you.

I have arranged a business trip to Tokyo that weekend and I can't reschedule it. I am expecting a promotion this year, so I really have to keep my head down.

You have always been amazingly supportive to me and I hate that I have to let you down this time. Please let me make it up to you.

I hope you have received my gift customized especially for you and that you like it. Also, I am sure it will be a lovely gathering and everything will be just perfect.

Lots of love,
Serena

親愛的 Jane，

我覺得好難過，我沒辦法參加你的生日派對。這是你的大日子，真是為你開心！多麼希望自己可以出席。

我那個週末安排要出差去東京，並且無法改期。我期盼今年能獲得升遷的機會，所以我要保持低調一點。

你一直都對我如此支持照顧，我真氣自己這次要讓你失望了，請讓我補償你吧！

我希望你已經有收到我特別為你客製化的禮物，希望你喜歡。還有，我相信這會是一個超棒的派對，而且每一件事情都會完美順利。

很多的愛，
Serena

❶ I wish I could be there for you.
真希望我能出席。

❷ I wish I could attend your fundraising dinner.
我真希望我可以參加你的募款晚宴。

❸ I am sorry for not being able to attend your fundraising dinner.
我很抱歉沒有出席你的募款晚宴。

❹ Unfortunately, I will be chairing a team building meeting **on the same day**.
真不巧，我那天要主持團隊激勵訓練會議。

❺ Please forgive me for missing your big opening.
請原諒我錯過你的盛大開幕。

❻ I hope you will visit me over the long weekend, and we can catch up.
希望你可以在連假的時候來找我，我們聚聚。

❼ Please convey my disappointment to your husband and wish him a lovely birthday. Let's go out for dinner next weekend.
請幫我轉達你先生我很抱歉，也幫我祝他生日快樂。我們下週末一起晚餐好嗎？

❽ I was at the hospital for a surgery. **I am extremely disappointed that** I couldn't be there.
我人在醫院接受手術，我也很難過我不能出席。

❾ I was looking forward to it, but I had to go out of town unexpectedly.
我本來很期待要去的，但是我突然要出城一趟。

⑩ My best wishes to your big opening.

祝福你開幕大順利。

make it up to someone　補償某人（因為讓對方失望或受到損失）

▶ I am sorry I didn't attend your party. Let me **make it up** to you.

很抱歉我沒去你的派對，讓我補償你吧。

❶ unexpectedly　突然地；出乎意料地

▶ Her parents showed up **unexpectedly**.

她的父母出乎大家意料地來了。

out of the blue　突然

▶ Our manager quit his job **out of blue**. Everyone was shocked.

我們經理突然毫無預警就辭職了，每個人都很驚訝。

❷ opening　（某事件、活動等）開幕會

▶ The department store's **opening** will take place this Saturday.

百貨公司的開幕會在這個星期六舉行。

LETTER ㉛ 向缺席活動道歉

223

How to Make a Healing Apology
如何表達一個真心誠意的道歉

道歉是一門藝術，最難的地方莫過於事件起因並非無心之過，而傷害已經造成，不是按下 "undo/unsend/recall（收回鍵）" 就可以一筆勾銷的。本帖道歉用語重點在告訴對方我們明白自己的錯誤，並且理解對方受到的傷害，才有可能進一步提出自己願意修補感情的誠意。

💬 **小提醒大領悟** Reminders

#對不起說了又能如何 #但還是要說

> 道歉的確不能只是紙上談兵，不過在許多尷尬的情境下，我們發現自己緊張到語塞說不出話時（tongue-tied），道歉信仍是很好的管道。

 書信寫作步驟 Step by Step

STEP 1 道歉

I am deeply sorry for being unfaithful, telling lies, and keeping endless secrets from you.
真的很對不起，我對你不忠誠、不斷撒謊、隱瞞很多祕密。

STEP 2　認知事實

I **palmed you off with** feeble excuses, again and again. That I twisted the knife (in the wound) shattered the foundation of trust and damaged our relationship.

我一次又一次用根本站不住腳的藉口打發你。我在你的傷口上灑鹽，摧毀了我們互信的基礎，嚴重傷害我們的關係。

STEP 3　修補關係

You do mean the world to me. I want to fix it although I don't even know how I can possibly earn your trust again.

你對我來說就是全世界。我想修補傷害，即使我根本無法想像我要如何再次贏得你的信任。

 情 境 Situation

你在電視台工作，你的朋友 Fiona 對於表演很有興趣，他請你幫忙把他自己拍的一個帶子轉給你的主管參考，看看有沒有表演機會，你當下答應了之後很後悔，因為你覺得你才剛進公司沒多久，做這件事情並不恰當，你怕尷尬就一直放著，禁不住朋友一直詢問，你只好對 Fiona 撒謊說主管認為不適合，其實你連那個帶子都沒有打開來看過。某日酒過三巡，Fiona 再度提起心中的疑問，你覺得自己很沒面子，竟然還指責對方不應該把你當成捷徑，造成你的困擾，Fiona 一氣之下當場離開……

Dear Fiona,

I am deeply sorry for being such an unfaithful friend. I promised to help you but sadly I didn't deliver. **I was ashamed to admit that** I lied to you, so I **palmed you off with** feeble excuses, again and again. I even twisted the knife by blaming you for all of this.

You are the one who always encourages me **"don't sell yourself short** and go for your dreams", but **when you needed me, I wasn't there**. I feel so terrible. What I have done totally shattered the foundation of trust and damaged our friendship. I don't even know how **I can possibly make it right**.

I do want to make everything better and am trying with all my heart. You will have plenty of time to see that I'm making it up to you.

Regretfully,
Serena

親愛的 Fiona，

我很抱歉成了如此不忠誠的朋友。我答應要幫你，很遺憾地卻沒做到。我又羞愧到不敢承認我欺騙你，所以只好用一堆爛藉口一再敷衍你。更糟的是，我還把這一切都怪罪到你頭上。

一直以來，你總是鼓勵我，「不要小看自己，勇敢追夢」，然而我卻在你需要我支持的時候辜負了你。我覺得糟透了。我所做的一切摧毀了我們互信的基礎，嚴重傷害我們的友誼，我甚至不知道我該怎麼讓一切和好如初。

我全心全意想讓事情好轉，我會讓你看見我的改變。

很抱歉地，
Serena

❶ I am so sorry for causing all the drama.
很抱歉我造成一片混亂。

❷ I am sorry for what I did to you and **there's no excuse for** my behavior.
我對我所做的事情感到非常抱歉,沒有任何藉口可以為我的行為開脫。

❸ **I can't tell how regretful I am**.
我真的非常後悔。

❹ **It was too painful to admit that** I hurt something precious that would probably never be healed.
我不知道該怎麼承認,我傷害了珍貴的東西,且或許永遠都無法被修補。

❺ My inappropriate behavior embarrassed you and your friends.
我不恰當的言行讓你跟你的朋友蒙羞。

❻ It is my fault. **I take the blame**.
是我的錯,我會承擔所有責任。

❼ I feel ashamed for what I have done.
我為自己所做的事情感到羞愧。

❽ **There's no excuse for** my behavior.
沒有任何藉口可以為我的行為開脫。

❾ I am sorry for being so flat-out careless and selfish. **It never occurred to me** that those things I said could offend you.
我很抱歉我竟然如此粗心大意與自私,我從來沒想過我說那些話會刺傷你。

LETTER ㉜ 如何表達一個真心誠意的道歉

⑩ I do know that "sorry" is an empty word and saying sorry isn't enough.

我真的知道「對不起」三個字是如此空洞無意，說抱歉更是沒有用處。

---

⑪ I shouldn't **have broken the promise** and I am so angry at myself for destroying something that was so beautiful and unique.

我不應該違背諾言，我對我自己非常生氣，竟然毀了這麼美好、獨特的感情。

慣用語與句型應用指南

❶ occur to someone that... （腦海裡）想到……；出現……的念頭

▶ The idea just **occurred to** me last night.
我昨天晚上冒出這個念頭。

▶ Does it ever **occur to** you **that** she's just not into you?
你有沒有想過她其實就沒那麼喜歡你？

---

❷ mean the world to someone 對某人來說是一切；非常重要

▶ His career **means the world to** him.
他的事業就是他的一切。

---

❸ sell someone/yourself short 低估、小看某人／自己

▶ Don't **sell yourself short**.
別看扁自己。

---

❹ take the blame 歸過失給自己；認錯

▶ I don't think that if anything goes wrong, she would **take the blame**.
我不認為如果出了問題，她會負責。

❺ twist/turn the knife (in the wound)
（讓已經難受的人）更加痛苦

▶ The bully horribly **twisted the knife** by laughing at the crippled kid.
惡霸譏笑那個跛腳的孩子，在他傷口上灑鹽。

單字片語應用指南

❶ be down with 結束

▶ **Are** you **down with** the washing machine?
你用完洗衣機了嗎？

▶ I **am** totally **down with** him.
我真的受夠他了。

❷ break/keep a promise 違背／遵守諾言

▶ She didn't realize that when she **broke** her **promise**, she broke more than just words.
她不知道當她違背諾言時，她違背的不只是說出口的那幾個字而已。

❸ drama 戲劇性的場面、事件

▶ After giving birth, she keeps dealing with some family **drama**.
在生產之後，她不斷的在處理家庭的戲劇化事件。

❹ feeble 虛弱的；無效的

▶ How can you do those things to such a **feeble** and helpless person?
你怎麼能對一個虛弱無助的人做出那些事情？

▶ Don't make a **feeble** excuse.
別說那種站不住腳的藉口。

❺ flat-out （副詞）絕對地；十足地（強調）

▶ Everything you told is just **flat-out** confusing.
你跟我說的每一件事情真的超級令人困惑的。

（形容詞）極端的；十足的（尤指不好的事）

▶ What she said was just a **flat-out** lie.
她說的完全就是一個謊言。

❻ palm...off 把不想要的人事物擺脫掉（通常包含欺騙）
"palm something off on someone"

▶ I can understand you hate it so much, but you can't just **palm** it **off on** someone else.
我知可以理解你很討厭這件事情，但是你不能就直接把事情推給別人承擔。

▶ My boss tried to **palm** the old car **off on** me.
我老闆試圖要（騙）我買下那輛舊車。

❼ take it back 收回（說錯的話）

▶ You can't **take back** what you have already said.
你不能收回你已經說出去的話。

❽ with all my heart 完全地

▶ I love her **with all my heart**.
我全心全意愛她。

Apology Letters to Friends or Family

寫給家人或朋友的道歉信（無心之過）

無心之過通常都可以被原諒，但是當這個無心的行為或是話語的確造成朋友間的不愉快，仍須妥善應對，才能經營長久又健康的人際關係。除了「對不起」三個字，還有什麼字可以表達你的歉疚之情呢？

 小提醒大領悟 Reminders

---

❶ **小心你的句子讓人覺得你在迴避事實**

像是政治人物常用的語言：**"If our mistake inconvenienced anyone, we are deeply sorry.**（如果我們的疏失造成任何人不便，我們深感抱歉。）"，這樣的句子讓人有種錯覺，好像如果沒人特別感到不舒服，就無須道歉了？或是你用 **"I am sorry if I hurt your feelings.**（如果我傷到你，很抱歉。）"，一樣都很容易讓道歉變成迴避事實。

❷ **無心之過的亮點在「解釋」上面**

有誠意的讓對方瞭解來龍去脈，無須過度渲染，否則又變得像在找藉口，因為畢竟對方的確有損失。解釋應當要清楚、簡潔、適度。

STEP 1　道歉

I apologize for my mistake. I should have let you know the unexpected venue change. **Being busy is never an excuse.**

對不起，我應該讓你知道突然改了地點。忙碌從來就不是藉口。

STEP 2　提及對方受到的損害，並提供解釋

How could I have possibly forgotten to tell you that the event had been rescheduled? I couldn't imagine how inconvenient and frustrating this whole situation has been for you.

我怎麼可能會忘記告訴你活動改時間了呢？我沒辦法想像這所有的情況對你來說有多不方便跟多令人灰心。

STEP 3　補救

You can rest assured that I will be more aware of my limits at work and won't let an overwhelming workload cause so much drama.

您可以放心，我會更注意自己在工作上的極限，不會再讓過度疲憊的狀態引起風波了。

你想把好幾群朋友拉在一起，在家裡舉辦一個露天烤肉派對。沒想到就在活動兩天前，家裡突然發生狀況，不適合舉辦派對，但是因為你工作很忙就沒有一一通知大家，決定到時等大家都到你家後，再一起步行到附近餐廳。結果當天竟然出了烏龍，好友 Amy 因為遲到所以完全在狀況外，頻頻在你家門口按門鈴，更不巧的是，她的手機竟然掉在 Uber 上，這下糗了⋯⋯

範 例 Example

Hi Amy,

I am sorry for causing the drama and leaving you in the lurch. I didn't tell everyone about the **last-minute venue change** because I thought that you guys would come to my house anyway. I was too careless. **I owe you an apology**.

It must be frustrating for you. I am so embarrassed to admit that **I could have managed things carefully**. I was so overwhelmed recently that I didn't handle an unexpected situation well. However, it was me that invited you so it's my responsibility to take care of everyone.

I sincerely apologize for my careless behavior that caused you inconvenience and disappointment. You mean a great deal to me, and I assure you, this won't happen again.

Lots of love,
Serena

LETTER **33** 寫給家人或朋友的道歉信（無心之過）

親愛的 Amy,

抱歉惹出這些風波，把你忘在一邊了。我沒有跟大家說臨時更改聚會地點，因為我想反正大家會先來我家，我真的很粗心。我欠你一個道歉。

你一定感到非常失落。我很汗顏的承認，我應該細心處理好這些事的。我最近真的是忙到不可開交，導致我對於這些突發狀況沒有妥善應對。不過，我到底是主辦人，照顧好每一位賓客是我的責任。

為了我粗心的行為，我誠摯的向你道歉，造成你的困擾不好意思。你對我來說非常重要，我跟你保證，這種事情不會再發生了。

很多的愛，
Serena

實用例句應用指南

❶ I am not making excuses for my behavior. Please don't misunderstand me.
我這不是在為我的行為找藉口，請別誤會我。

❷ We were deeply regretful and shocked when we realized that we forgot to send you an invitation. **It was an unfortunate oversight**.
我們感到非常懊悔以及不敢置信，我們竟然忘了寄邀請函給你。這真是一個令人遺憾的疏漏。

❸ The event was just not complete without you. I wish I would have found out sooner that you didn't receive the invitation.
這個活動沒有你就不完整了，我真希望我能早一點發現你沒有收到邀請函。

❹ I realized, **to my dismay**, that I had overlooked you on the guest list. It's a stupid mistake but an unintentional one.
我很沮喪的發現我竟然把你從客人名單中漏掉了，這真是一個愚蠢的錯誤，但卻不是有意的。

❺ I apologize for my careless behavior that caused you inconvenience and pain.
為了我的粗心大意造成你的不便與痛苦，跟你致歉。

❻ My sincere apologies for missing our appointment.
我忘記我們有約，對此我誠心的道歉。

❼ I am deeply sorry for my mistake.
我真的很抱歉犯了這個錯誤。

慣用語與句型應用指南

❶ **leave someone in the lurch** 　丟下、撇下某人不管
▶ His parents **left** him **in the lurch** when he needed them.
他父母在他需要他們的時候撇下他不管。

❷ **sorry about that** 　道歉（用在較為無傷大雅的事情）
▶ I forgot to call you last night. **Sorry about that**.
我昨天晚上忘記打給你，對不起。

❸ **to one's surprise / dismay / disappointment...**
令某人感到驚訝 / 沮喪 / 失望……
to one's 後面加上各種情緒名詞，用來表示感受。
▶ **To** my **surprise**, she was pretty calm.
我很驚訝，她竟然這麼冷靜。
▶ **To** our **disappointment**, the game was canceled.
我們感到非常失望，比賽被取消了。

❶ blunder （尤指欠考慮、粗心所釀成的）大錯

▶ I made a **blunder** at work and it's really unprofessional.
我在工作上犯了一個非常不專業的大錯。

❷ dismay （不可數名詞）沮喪；灰心；失望

▶ They have been filled with **dismay** by the tragedy.
因為這個悲劇，他們感到非常難過。

▶ The refugee watched with **dismay** as flames engulfed everything.
難民看著大火吞噬一切，感到萬分難過。

❸ embarrassed 尷尬；害羞；不好意思

▶ I was too **embarrassed** to admit that I cheated on the exam.
我不好意思承認我考試作弊。

❹ make excuses 找理由；編藉口

▶ You can't always **make excuses** for your mistakes.
你不能總是替自己犯的錯誤找藉口。

❺ overlook 忽略；忽視；沒注意到

▶ We all should learn to **overlook** friends and family's minor faults.
我們都應該學著忽略家人與朋友的小過錯。

❻ oversight 失察；疏忽

▶ The officials claimed that it's an **oversight** and would never happen again.
官員聲稱這只是一次小失誤，而且不會再發生。

How to Say No to Someone (Even Your Best Friend)
如何拒絕某人（甚至是你最好的朋友）

朋友間的提議、要求各式各樣，比如說想跟你借你新買的車、借錢週轉。這種時刻要對朋友說「不」，該如何啟齒？如何堅持自己的原則，又不會傷了感情呢？

 小提醒大領悟 Reminders

#未讀訊息的暗示

社群網站訊息流通的便利性，再加上大家手機不離身的習慣，都讓我們回覆訊息之前的「猶豫期」變得敏感，即使你不把訊息打開想避開已讀不回的尷尬，其實對對方來說，這跟已讀不回其實也差不了太多。如果想要多一點緩衝時間，不如用比較溫和的句子，像 "Hey, I'll get back to you.（我確認一下再回你。）" 或 "Sorry, I'm afraid I won't be free, but not sure. Let me get back to you!（我那天好像抽不開身耶，但是不確定，我確認過後再回你！）"

 書信寫作步驟 Step by Step

STEP 1　表達自己其實很願意

That **sounds like a good idea** and I'd love/like to join you.
聽起來很讚，我很樂意幫忙。

STEP 2　各種「誠實」的理由

Unfortunately, I'm afraid I won't be free this weekend. I have a hectic schedule.

不巧的是，我這個週末行程滿滿，我恐怕沒辦法。

STEP 3　提供備案或是各種建議

I get the sense there's something you want to discuss. I'd love to help you come up with a plan.

我覺得你可能很想要找人討論，我可以協助你一起想個辦法。

 情 境 Situation

朋友 Cathy 發訊息給你，想邀你幫忙籌備 Bake For Charity（為公益募款烘焙）的活動，你覺得時間上忙不過來，而且你對這個活動也沒什麼興趣，但是你之前在學校舉辦台灣週的活動，Cathy 很認真地在自己的社群網站上大力幫你宣傳。你思索著要如何回信才不會太掃興……

 範 例 Example

Hey Cathy,

It's very nice of you to devote your time and effort to this event. I would definitely be there if I could. I'm sorry that I am so busy preparing for the finals and term papers.

But I would love to support you in a different way. I'd love to chip in ￡30 for the cake you plan to make. Thank you for being such a wonderful friend. Good luck with the event! I know you're going to do a terrific job.

Best,
Serena

嗨 Cathy，

你花時間和精力投入這個活動真的很不錯。我如果可以加入，一定會幫忙。我很抱歉我真的超級分身乏術，因為我在忙著準備期末考跟期末報告。

但是我很樂意用不同的方式支持你，我想為你計畫做蛋糕的費用，分擔三十英鎊。謝謝你總是當一個這麼完美的朋友，祝你的活動一切順利！我相信你一定可以做得很棒。

祝好，
Serena

實用例句應用指南

❶ **I'm flattered that** you'd like to **pick my brain.**
你認為我的意見能帶來幫助，真讓我受寵若驚。

❷ You know how much I love your parties.
你知道我多愛你的派對。

❸ **It's very nice of** you to arrange this.
你花時間安排這些事情真好。

❹ **The last thing I would do** is to say no to you.
我最不想做的事情就是拒絕你。

❺ I am sorry that I can't make it right now but will let you know when and if I can.
我很抱歉我現在不行，但如果可以的話，我就會跟你說。

❻ But I realized I had been **spreading myself too thin**.
但是我發現我實在是分身乏術。

❼ But I would love to have you two over for drinks sometime.
但我想找時間請你們兩個來喝一杯。

❽ Honestly, I've never really had a conversation with Sammy. I think I'll just wish him a happy birthday in person.
老實說，我跟 Sammy 沒有真的講過話。我想我再當面祝他生日快樂就好了。

❾ **Why don't you** go to the beach instead?
你們何不改成去海邊啊？

❿ **Do/Would you mind if we** reschedule our event? How about next week?
如果我們的活動改期，你會介意嗎？下禮拜如何？

⓫ If **I were** you, I would ask Sammy.
如果我是你的話，我會去問 Sammy。

慣用語與句型應用指南

❶ I am afraid... （委婉地）說出壞消息、與對方期望相反的事情
▶ **I'm afraid** you have misunderstood my arguments.
恐怕你誤會我的意見了。

❷ If I were... I would...
如果我是⋯⋯的話，我會⋯⋯；建議某人做某事、決定
▶ **If I were** you, **I would** study harder.
如果我是你的話，我會用功一點。

► **If I were** her, **I would** tell the truth.
如果我是她的話，我會說出事實。

❸ **It's very nice/kind of someone** 某人很好心、善意

► **It's very kind of** you to invite me to your housewarming party.
你邀請我參加喬遷派對，真的很窩心。

❹ **spread yourself too thin**
同一時間做太多事情（以至沒有時間、精神好好關注任何一件事情）

► I realized that I had been **spreading myself too thin** so I made the decision to get my priorities right.
我知道我把自己逼到不行了，所以我決定要把優先順序抓出來。

❺ **the last thing/person**
最後一件事情／一個人；最不想、最不願意做／找的事情／人

► **The last thing** I wanted was to fail you.
我最不想做的就是讓你失望。

► Mark is **the last person** I would trust with my keys.
我最不放心把鑰匙交給 Mark 保管。

單字片語應用指南

❶ **flatter** 感到榮幸；（被稱讚、奉承）感到高興

► We were all **flattered** to be invited to her party.
我們感到很榮幸被邀請參加她的派對。

❷ **hectic** 繁忙的

► The manager has a **hectic** schedule this week.
經理本週行程滿檔。

LETTER ㉟

How to Decline an Invitation to Dinner or Other Social Events

如何拒絕一頓晚餐或社交活動的邀請

當你必須拒絕朋友邀請的聚會，尤其當此類邀約多半是同喜同樂之事，除非你是打算這個人最好永遠不要再約你，否則不能只說 "I can't go because of a prior commitment.（我不能去，因為已經有約了。）" 而已。

小提醒大領悟 Reminders

❶ 從「不好意思」到「我很遺憾」

拒絕的用字口氣，可以用邀請出席的活動類別來判斷。如果那是對方人生中無比重要或是一生只有一次的事情，比如說婚喪喜慶，你無法出席等於永遠錯過了，感到遺憾等字眼就必須表達出來。

❷ 既然要拒絕，千萬不要拖

或許你因為一開始覺得尷尬而想晚點再回，沒想到事情一忙就忘了，反而把情況弄得更糟，讓人覺得你既然不能來為何不早說。如果你不確定自己到時是否可以出席，更要清楚說出來，讓對方有應變處理的心理準備。

STEP 1　感謝對方的邀請以及用心

Thank you so much for inviting me and I do think it would be a very nice thing to get together.

謝謝你邀請我，我真的覺得大家聚聚很棒。

STEP 2　表達遺憾後悔

I wish I could say yes, but it's almost impossible for me during the week.

我很想去，但是這禮拜對我來說幾乎不可能。

STEP 3　提供具體的解釋

I am swamped with work and really stressed out.

我被工作壓得喘不過氣，壓力非常大。

STEP 4　斟酌提供意見幫忙或是轉圜方案

Is it okay if I visit you next weekend instead?

如果我下個週末去找你呢？

 情 境 Situation

你的朋友 Susan 寄信邀請你參加她精心籌備的「殺人案解謎晚餐會（Murder Mystery Party）」，你跟幾個好朋友的確有一陣子沒有相聚了，可是你最近真的是忙到厭世，不僅抽不開身，也沒有體力跟心情與會，可是你也不想用「很忙」潦草交代……

Hi Susan,

Thank you for arranging the get-together. It's very sweet of you and a Murder Mystery Party sounds fantastic and FUN. Sadly, I am so swamped with work this week and really stressed out. I just survived the hell-like final exams and I still have two proposals to go before the end of this month.

I think I'll pass this time, although I really want to be there and it surely would be so great to meet all our friends.

Let me be the host next time, to make it up to you, PLEASE!

Miss you,
Serena

嗨 Susan,

謝謝你操心舉辦聚會,而且謀殺案解謎晚餐耶,感覺超好玩、超棒的! 但我好慘,我這週深陷作業,壓力超大。我才剛從期末地獄活過來, 然後還有兩份企劃書要在月底前生出來。

我想我這次就先不參加了,雖然我真的很想出席,跟大家同樂一定超 棒的!

下次換我主辦,補償大家,拜託!

想念你們的,
Serena

❶ You have a big heart.
你人真的很好。

❷ I think I am going to pass.
我想我這次就不參加了。

❸ **If I could make it, I definitely would, but I have promised** Lisa to spend the weekend in Paris.
如果我可以去，我一定會去的，可惜我先答應 Lisa 要陪她去巴黎度週末了。

❹ **I am feeling a bit under the weather** and not very comfortable.
我感冒了，現在不太舒服。

❺ I am (busy) planning for the college entrance exam and **it has completely drained me**.
我為了大學入學考試忙得不可開交，已經累爆了。

❻ I wish I could be there! Can't wait to hear about it!
真希望我可以出席！等不急之後聽你說聚會的情形！

❼ I am busy with **a myriad of activities** – [thing A, B, C...]
我因為超多事情很忙碌——[列舉幾項：A、B、C……]。

❽ **I already have plans for that night**.
我那天晚上已經有活動安排了。

❾ Let me know how I can help in a different way.
跟我說我可以幫什麼忙。

❿ Maybe another time?
也許改天？

慣用語與句型應用指南

❶ have a big heart （人）善良、慷慨。

▶ My grandmother **has a big heart**.
我奶奶為人慷慨。

big-hearted （形容詞）文意同上

▶ She is **big-hearted**.
她很慷慨善良。

★同義字：**a heart of gold**（金子一樣的心）
反義字：**a heart of stone**（頑石一樣的心）

❷ be swamped with... 深陷於……

▶ We **are swamped with** work and can't take the time to listen to each other.
我們忙於工作而沒有心力去傾聽對方。

★ **swamp** 的名詞是「沼澤地」的意思。

單字片語應用指南

❶ drain （動詞）使疲憊

▶ The long journey has almost **drained** me.
這次長途旅行簡直把我累垮了。

（名詞）疲憊；負擔

▶ I think taking care of two babies is a big **drain** on her energy.
我覺得照顧兩個嬰兒對她來說非常吃力。

❷ **myriad** （名詞）很大數量

▶ We've got a **myriad** of choices.
我們有很多可以選擇。

---

❸ **under the weather** 感冒不適

字面上翻譯看起來像是在天氣之下，沒有道理，別搞錯囉。

▶ I am feeling a bit **under the weather** so I called in sick.
我有點感冒了所以我打電話請假。

💬 **娜娜老師的寫作小撇步**

各種派對的說法：

▶ housewarming party 喬遷派對

▶ farewell party 歡送會

▶ surprise party 驚喜會

▶ bachelor party 告別單身漢派對

▶ bachelorette party 告別單身女郎派對

▶ dinner party 晚宴餐會

▶ sleepover party 過夜派對

▶ murder mystery party 謀殺案解謎晚餐

Sorry, but You Have Crossed the Line...

抱歉，但你踩到我的底線了……

有些朋友好像不太清楚「界線」，從幫他個小忙到動不動就把你當萬事通，或是不斷重複做出你不喜歡的事情，即使明示暗示他們都依然故我，讓我們頻頻翻白眼（roll your eyes）這時候免不了要「說清楚講明白」。然而淺詞用字該如何拿捏，才能達到目的又不會顯得過於嚴厲，或是造成無法挽回的傷害呢？

 小提醒大領悟 Reminders

#麻煩是怎麼開始的？

你知道嗎？在信件結尾加上 "Keep me posted.（讓我知道後續情況。）" 或 "I hope it helps.（希望這對你有幫助。）" 會帶給對方不同的兩個世界。如果你一開始就打算點到為止，請不用太過熱心的把模板句"Keep me posted."當作貼圖一樣放在信件末尾，可以用"I hope it helps."委婉的畫上句點。

 書信寫作步驟 Step by Step

STEP 1 委婉開頭

I just want you to know that I value our friendship so much and you are one of my best friends.

我想讓你知道，我重視我們的友誼，而你是我最好的朋友之一。

STEP 2　點出讓你感到不愉快的事實

I don't feel comfortable when you complain about our mutual friend Sammy. I hate to be caught in the middle, sorry.

每次你抱怨我們共同的朋友 Sammy，我的感受很不好。我不喜歡被夾在中間，抱歉。

STEP 3　結尾（稍微安慰對方／給對方台階下／重申你在意的問題）

I know you didn't mean it and I hope you won't take it the wrong way. The thing is, you both are my friends and I can't take sides.

我知道你其實沒有那個意思，而且我不想要你誤會我。重點是，你們兩個都是我的朋友，而我不能選邊站。

 情 境 Situation

你收到一則通知，是朋友傳來的訊息，說他在跟他的大學同學吃飯時提到你，他大學同學正準備轉換跑道，而你朋友過度熱心的直接替對方問你有沒有空跟他見面聊一下，分享你在行銷領域多年的經驗，你當下覺得有點不自在。其實這種狀況已經不只一次，之前幾次你都忍著不說，這次實在很不高興⋯⋯

Hey Jason,

We have been friends for such a long time. I value our friendship so I have to be honest with you. I feel frustrated when you want me to help a "friend", whom I barely know, without even asking me. I didn't mean that I don't want to help your friends. What I care about is that you come to me first before you promise others. Otherwise, I feel awkward and embarrassed.

Don't take it the wrong way. I know you didn't mean it and I don't blame you, I just hope you understand.

Best,
Serena

嗨 Jason，

我們當朋友這麼久了，我很重視我們的友情，所以我要坦誠告訴你，我覺得很無奈，每次你請我幫一個我根本不認識的「朋友」，也不事先問我。我的意思不是不願意幫助你的朋友，我在意的是，你應該在答應別人之前先來問我，不然，我覺得好尷尬、很不舒服。

不要誤會我的意思，我知道你不是故意的，我也不是在責怪你什麼，我只是希望你可以理解。

祝好，
Serena

❶ Recently, I am feeling overwhelmed. You might find the following books helpful.

最近我真的忙得不可開交，你可能會覺得以下的書目對你有幫助。

---

❷ I am sorry that I think I will never be able to help you if you always ask for a favor at the last minute.

我很抱歉，我覺得如果你每次都是到最後一刻才來請我幫忙，我可能永遠都無法幫你的忙。

---

❸ **Don't take it the wrong way**. I'm just not comfortable sharing details of my private life.

別誤會，我只是不太喜歡談論我的私事。

---

❹ I feel uncomfortable when you [V], I'd like you to stop [Ving].

我不喜歡你 [做（某事）]，我希望你不要再 [這麼做]。

---

❺ It's really frustrating for me when you [V].

每當你 [做（某事）] 的時候，我真的覺得很無奈。

---

❻ I want to let you know that I value our time together very much and that's why it upsets me that you always **have a hard time** being punctual.

我想讓你知道，我很珍惜我們相聚的時光，這也是為什麼每次你都無法準時讓我蠻難受的。

慣用語與句型應用指南

❶ cross the line （行為）越過界限

▶ You really **crossed the line** this time.

你這次真的太過分了。

LETTER **36** 抱歉，但你踩到我的底線了……

251

❷ have a hard time　很難去做到某事

▶ I'm **having a hard time** trusting you.
我真的很難去相信你。

❸ in the middle　一個令人不舒服的尷尬處境；夾在中間、左右為難

▶ Sammy was caught **in the middle** when her parents got divorced.
Sammy 的父母離婚時，她夾在中間覺得很不好受。

❹ take something the wrong way
誤解、誤會，造成被冒犯或不愉快的感受

▶ Don't **take it the wrong way**. I just don't like to talk about my private life.
別誤會我的意思，我只是不喜歡談論我的私事。

❺ take sides　選一邊支持；（在兩方爭執之中）表明立場

▶ I refused to **take sides** on the issue.
我拒絕在這個議題上表明我支持哪一方。

❻ The thing is, ...　（解釋、藉口的開頭）事情是這樣的，……

▶ I am sorry I didn't get back to you. **The thing is**, I was so busy with work last week.
對不起我沒有回你電話。事情是這樣的，我上禮拜工作非常忙。

SORRY 對不起

❶ I didn't mean to... 我不是有意／故意這麼做

❷ leave the door open for... 不排除……的可能性

❸ please give my regards to someone
請代我問候某人

❹ make it up to someone 補償某人

❺ sell somebody/yourself short
低估、小看某人／自己

❻ take the blame 歸過失給自己；認錯

❼ twist/turn the knife (in the wound)
（讓已經難受的人）更加痛苦

❽ leave someone in the lurch 丟下、撇下某人不管

❾ spread yourself too thin 同一時間做太多事情

❿ have a big heart （人）善良、慷慨

⓫ have a hard time 很難去做到某事

⓬ take something the wrong way
誤解、誤會造成被冒犯或不愉快的感受

#請 #謝謝 #對不起
好禮貌運動的這三位是從哪裡冒出來的？

If you please...

是個古老並且正式的「煩請對方」的用法，當你提出某些動作要求，比如說 Follow me（跟著我），但你並不是在給對方指令（order），自然會加上：「如果你願意的話，麻煩你跟著我，我將會……（Follow me, if you please and I will...）」，換言之，這個「如果你願意的話」意味著，其實你知道對方完全沒有義務要這麼做（they are under no obligation to do this）。不過，真實生活上的使用情境千變萬化，簡短的一個 Please（請）字，很多時候也不一定是要表達我們真的完全「尊重」對方的意思，有時候反而是說話者想要顯現出自己的氣度或禮貌，即使對方的行為似乎應該如此，我們還是會選擇說 "Please"。

▶ **Please** submit your homework by Monday.
  煩請於星期一前交出你的作業。

▶ Be kind to your little brother, **please**!
  麻煩對你弟弟好一點！

▶ **Would you please** stop making the noises during the class?
  可以請你不要在課堂上製造噪音了嗎？

Thanks

Thank 這個字是從古英文 thanc：thought 而來，也跟拉丁文 tongere：to know 有關聯。人類社會掛在口頭上表示禮貌的這個 Thanks 其實意思跟 Think 也有相似之處呢！想想，當別人幫助了你，你會告訴他：「我會把你對我的好記在心裡的」，這是多麼有誠意的表示呢！"Thanks = I will always remember what you did for me." 不過在今時代使用上，Thanks 已經變成像是一般口頭禪的存在，到底說謝謝的時候心裡是不是有連結到 "Think" 就是個未知數囉！另外這個字也可用來反諷成「真謝謝你喔！」的說法，跟感恩的心一點關係都沒有喔！

▶ **Thank** you for telling mom I didn't finish the homework before I go out.
謝謝你告訴媽我還沒寫完功課就跑出去玩喔。

▶ Right, right. **Thanks** for sharing with me, but I have to go now. See you.
好、好，謝謝你跟我分享，但我必須走了，掰。

▶ **Thank** you for being honest to me, but I'd rather not know the truth.
謝謝你對我坦白，但我寧願不知道事實為何。

Sorry

從古英文 Sar：sore（痛）而來，會道歉都是因為我讓你「痛」了。Apology 不是一直以來都表示 Sorry 的意思的，如果回溯到 16 世紀，你碰到的 apology 應該都會是指「辯解、辯護」之意，而不是要跟誰道歉。那到底什麼時候 apology 才開始代表 "I am sorry" 的意思呢？這可能都得歸到莎士比亞的頭上了，根據韋氏字典以及牛津字典的考證，雖然或許有可能更早之前就有這樣的使用，不過莎士比亞的 *Richard III*《理查三世》裡面，這句話就告訴大家 Apology 跟 Sorry 終於走到一起："My lord, there needs no such apologie（我的主人，不需要這樣道歉）"。到現在 sorry 也同 thanks 一樣，依照句意會成反諷的意味。

▶ **Sorry** not sorry.
抱歉不抱歉，沒有歉意的意思。

▶ Oops, **sorry**. I didn't mean to do it.
喔抱歉，我不是故意的。

▶ **Sorry** but I think you are overreacted.
抱歉，但我覺得你反應過度了。

國家圖書館出版品預行編目 (CIP) 資料

日常英文書信寫作指南：在職場無往不利、在朋友圈有求必應的36堂寫作課 / 娜娜老師著. -- 初版.
-- 桃園市：前進出版, 2019.08
　面；　公分
ISBN 978-986-97365-4-1（平裝）

1.英語 2.寫作法 3.商業書信

805.171　　　　　　　　　　　108010369

日常英文書信寫作指南

在職場無往不利、在朋友圈
有求必應的 36 堂寫作課

書名 / 日常英文書信寫作指南：在職場無往不利、在朋友圈有求必應的 36 堂寫作課
作者 / 娜娜老師
繪圖 / Teng
總編輯 / 常祈天
編輯 / 江藝榕
校對 / Daniel Elliott
封面設計 / 小陳
視覺設計 / 楊雅屏
內文排版 / 黃雅芬
印製 / 金濱印刷事業有限公司

出版 / 前進出版有限公司
地址 / 桃園市龜山區文青路 163 號 10 樓之五
電話 /（03）397-8360

初版一刷 / 2019 年 08 月
定價 / 新台幣 299 元 / 港幣 100 元

台灣總經銷 / 易可數位行銷股份有限公司
地址 / 新北市新店區寶橋路 235 巷 6 弄 3 號 5 樓
電話 /（02）8911-0825

港澳總經銷 / 和平圖書有限公司
地址 / 香港柴灣嘉業街 12 號百樂門大廈 17 樓
電話 /（852）2804-6687
傳真 /（852）2804-6409